Tomorrow's Sun

PAUL GARVEY

ISBN:
ISBN-13: 978-1482514834
ISBN-10: 1482514834

DEDICATION

For My Family

1 DERAILED

Billy served from '76 – '80 in the U.S. army. They put him in airborne. He didn't mind, as far as he was concerned, this was just a means to an end. The army was going to write his ticket. He never wanted to be a soldier. He joined up for one reason and one reason only. He read that once you served in the army they'd set you up with enough money to put you through college. All Billy ever wanted to do was go to college and do something . . . anything . . . to prove to himself that he was better than his surroundings. He wanted to prove to everyone else that you don't have to come from something to be something.

Two things happened while home on leave in December '79 though. First, Billy spent the night with on again off again girlfriend Kathleen Carroll, and second, the Soviets invaded Afghanistan.

Kathleen fell pregnant for the first time - Immaculate Conception her catholic parents would've had you believe. Billy's dreams faded to the background after that. The army begged him to re-enlist. He refused. With the Russians in Afghanistan it was only a matter of time before the U.S. got into the mix. Going to war was never really an issue for Billy. He felt it would've been naïve on his part to join the military without considering the aspect that at some point his country could send him off to fight. But the way he saw it, he did his time, he didn't have to go to war, no point in re-joining. He didn't feel that he missed out on something. Plus, with a baby on the way he felt all his priorities shift inside him. Keeping the life safe that he helped bring into the world was his new focus.

The original plan, college, took a back seat then too. In those days, parents didn't willingly push their kids into college and rush to bear the brunt of six-figure loans so they could get shit-faced and explore with soft drugs for seven months out of the year. Well, maybe they did, but not around Billy's neighborhood.

In the Boston neighborhoods, more often than

not, if you're a boy you're a carpenter. If you're a girl, and you can afford two years of college, then you're a nurse. Unless of course, you had one of several Irish American last names that entitled you to the wonderful world of civil service. In which case, you could luck out as a cop or fireman and if you were really clever, a politician.

Billy didn't have the right name and unfortunately he couldn't hit a nail with a hammer if his life was on the line. Instead he worked over at the electric supply store on the Quincy-Dorchester Line under Neponset Bridge.

When he left the army a friend of his set him up with a job in the warehouse. He started off loading the pipe bays and driving the forklift, but soon worked his way up to the front desk. Nick McNulty, an old neighborhood friend managed the place and he knew Billy was a smart, hardworking guy, so he had no problem helping him out.

Nick McNulty took the reins of Neponset River Electric Supply from his uncle at the age of 22. His father's brother owned and operated the place for 40 years or so and once he felt comfortable doing so, he let Nick run the show. Nick worked in the warehouse since birth pretty much, so taking over at the front desk wasn't much of a leap. Plus, he had a way with people. He spent his formative years loading trucks with 10 foot long four inch galvanized pipe, which explained why he had to walk sideways through most doorways.

He epitomized Boston's working class, born to second generation Irish American, Catholic parents. He went to St. Ann's for Mass every Sunday as a kid and graduated from Catholic Memorial in West Roxbury. He grew up down the street from the family business on Neponset Avenue, never really left Boston or at least not New England. Then again, he never really wanted to either. He married his teenage sweetheart at 19 and had a baby girl by the age of 21. All in all, Nick was happy.

Summer Early 1980's

Nick pulled his mustang into the parking lot behind Gerard's corner store and threw it into park. Every morning the parking lot was full to the brim with pick-up trucks and vans while the laborers, painters and carpenters of Boston grabbed their breakfast and morning coffees. It was also the waiting area for legions of immigrants, formerly Irish, although nowadays guys from everywhere including Brazil, Mexico, even Haiti looking for a day's work.

They stand ready each morning with hammers and paint brushes in hand, hoping to get picked.

Nick let a Stones' song play out on the radio before killing the ignition. He and Billy went to open their doors just as the sky opened up. The last two or three days had been well into the 90's and humid like a Brazilian rainforest. That day in particular had been the worst yet. There's nothing anyone can do on days like that except stay in the shade and do your best to not move. If you step outside even for a second you look like you jumped in a lake, just soaked head to toe in sweat.

Sitting in the car just as the roar of thunder hit and raindrops the size of tennis balls began pounding the windscreen, Billy thought to himself how much he hated the heat and humidity, but he absolutely loved the relief that came with a thunderstorm. "Well, as long as you're not stuck in it," he thought. Within minutes you could feel the degrees just tick off the temperature and all of a sudden it's easy to breathe again. He turned to Nick with a smirk said, 'You wanna make a run for it?'

Nick nodded and said, 'On my count Sergeant . . . 1 . . . 2 . . . 3.' The two men jumped out of the Mustang and raced through the parking lot trying to avoid the massive puddles that had accumulated within seconds of the rain starting.

They ran across the street through the stopped traffic and entered the bar through the door on the right side. The local pub in Dorchester was like watching the opening scenes on Cheers. You could almost hear the theme song as soon as the door closed behind you.

The walls were lined with sports memorabilia, autographed Sox shirts and action shots of Phil Esposito and Bobby Orr. The familiar barmen stood behind the bar, washing down the counter, cleaning out glasses, wearing their short-sleeve button down shirts and black aprons. The patron's, mainly men ranging from ages 21 to 71, were scattered throughout the bar. They were spread out amongst the bar stools, wooden tables to the left, ceramic tables and benches to the right. This place was where the generation gap closed.

Billy walked up the bar and he and Nick took the two remaining seats right before the men's room – easy access. He gave the bartender, Tommy Stuart, a nod and turned to Nick, 'What're ya gonna have?'

Nick struggled to fit himself between the bar and the stool and answered, 'That depends, you staying for whole game or just popping in?'

'Kathleen and her parents took the boys up to New Hampshire for the weekend, so I can hang for a while". Billy thought again and said, "Who am I kidding, she'll be calling the house before she goes to bed, so I'd better be home before midnight or she'll use my nuts as a speed bag.'

Nicky laughed heartily, and slapped the bar with his open hand.

Billy yelled to the barman, 'Tommy, two pints and two shots of Jameson . . . on Nicky's tab.'

Nick shot Billy a look with a raised eyebrow. 'On me then huh? Whatever you sonofabitch. Hey, did you watch the Sox last night? Decent game.'

'Nah I had to help her pack up everything. I swear to God, for little people, the kids need a shit load of supplies – no pun intended.'

'Yah no kidding, my Julia's just over a year old and I gotta hire a fucking u-haul just to go to Nantasket beach.'

'Hahaha . . . That's a riot.' Billy laughed.

'What . . . the U-Haul?' Nick asked and looked pleased with himself.

'Nah Nicky . . . your fat ass at the beach'

Tommy the barman put the drinks on the bar.

'Here you go fellas, two loaves a bread and your milk to wash it down. It's on your tab Nicky.'

Nick looked at Billy again, 'He thought you were serious'

Billy answered with a smirk, 'What? You're good for it, what's the problem?'

Tommy laughed and said, 'I'll tell ya the problem, his fucking tab's so long, people mistake it for a roll of toilet paper.'

Nick flipped Tommy off and said 'F-off Tommy, I had to beg my uncle to put a word in to get you this job. Bout fucking time anyway, didn't know you had to personally fly over to Dublin every time someone orders a Guinness'.

Tommy thought better of any verbal retaliation and took that one on the chin.

Billy and Nick held down the fort in the two corner stools at the bar the whole night. It was the best view of the TV, plus there was no getting up to go the bar for drinks. They made it to the 7th inning of the Red Sox game before Nick started to nod his head. One shot wouldn't cut it for him. He had to go for a shot and a beer each round for the whole night. Billy took it pretty easy. Ever since Jimmy, his second son was born, he'd done his best to avoid getting stupidly drunk.

Billy saw Nick nod again for about the 5th time in a minute and said, 'Hey, Nick, you about ready to take off, we'll split a cab. I'll even walk it, it ain't that bad out.'

'Yeah, let me hit the men's room first though. Then we'll go.'

Tommy poked his head out from the other side of the bar and yelled over to Bill, 'Hey Billy, you got a phone call, it's your brother. I ain't your goddamn secretary'

Billy was searching in his pockets for a few dollar bills to leave a tip when Tommy got his attention. He looked over at Tommy with a confused face and said, 'What . . . which brother?'

Tommy gave him a shrug and showed him his palms, "How would I know. Here, come around and grab it. Don't touch the fucking taps."

Billy jumped from his stool and ducked under the bar. Before taking the phone he says, 'What the fuck do I want with your taps?'

He put the phone to his ear. 'Hello?'

'Bill'

'Yeah, what's up, Wally?' Billy cradled the phone between his ear and shoulder and fished again for tip money in his wallet.

'Ah Billy man . . . I need your fucking help man.'

'What, what's up Wally, what happened?'

Wally answered, his voice cracked when he said 'It isn't me Bill . . . It's John . . . I . . . he ain't answering. I mean, he ain't responding.'

Billy scanned the room and hooked his arm around the phone for privacy. 'Where the hell are you? I'm on the way, tell me where you are.'

'You're not going to like it man'

Bill yelled into the phone, 'Fucking tell me where you are!' About half of the people in the bar turned to look at him.

'I'm up the street Billy. Newhall Ave. Number 14'

'Stay there, I'm coming now. Stay there, don't fucking move!'

Billy slammed the receiver back on the hook. He ducked back under the bar and ran into the men's room. He yelled, 'Nicky! Where are you? I need your keys'.

Nick stumbled out of the stall. 'What, you nuts? You ain't taking the mustang.'

Billy grabbed Nick by the collar. 'Nicky, this is an emergency, something happened to my brother John. He's unconscious up on Newhall Ave.'

Nick looked at Billy with dismay, grabbed the keys from his pocket and handed them to Billy. 'Here man, go. I'll make my own way home, keep it for tonight.'

Billy shouldered his way through the front entrance of the bar, which was wedged tight at that point with red faced builders and painters still in overalls and slurring their speech. Their mesh of regional Irish accents sounded even less like actual words than usual, although Billy did hear one or two 'what the fucks' pretty clearly as he pushed and shoved his way through the crowd. He popped out of the doorway so hard he almost stumbled into the middle of Adams Street. He dropped to a knee just in front of the curb and scrambled to his feet in a split second. He bolted across the street, dodging a Ford pickup truck whose driver managed to brake and cut the wheel at the last second.

Billy hustled through the parking lot fumbling for the key to the car door that kept slipping from his grip like soap from a wet hand in the bath tub. The rain that held off for most of the Sox game came back with a vengeance, like it needed to make up for the hours of peace and kindness to the Fenway faithful.

He reached the driver's door and managed to work Nick's trick lock without trouble. He let the engine roar and spun out of the pot-holed parking lot lucky to keep all four tires intact. The mustang whipped a left turn down Minot Street to the corner and barely paused before taking a sharp right on two wheels and barreling up the street. He headed straight for the lights and might as well have been driving the General Lee as he took a right with the head of the car while the back end fish-tailed for a hundred yards down Ashmont Street. He rode gravity down the hill and swung a right onto Newhall Avenue, a narrow side street off the main road. He avoided a line of parked cars and jumped a curb on the left side of the street in front of the address his brother gave him.

In one fluid motion Billy pulled the emergency brake and leapt out of the driver's seat. He raced up the front steps to number 14, prepared to throw his shoulder through the door until his brother Walter pulled the front door open.

Billy paused, taken aback by the pale whiteness of Walter's face. He regained his composure after a moment and rushed through the doorway and heard Walter yell in a feeble voice behind him, 'straight through to the kitchen Billy'.

Billy's knees buckled when he saw him. John's pallid color made Walter's face look like he was blushing. John's eyes were closed and he had something that looked and smelled like vomit all down his shirt. Billy knelt beside him and touched John's face. The cold feeling made him shiver. He shrugged it off and put his right arm under John's knees and his left slung under his arms and upper back. He stood up straight and took a moment to get his balance. Billy walked gingerly through the hall careful to avoid hitting John's head off the walls in the narrow passage. He reached the front porch and yelled to Walter, "Wally, open the door of the car and get in the back so I can pass him through".

Still cradling John's fragile body, Billy ducked into the backseat and knelt on the floor of the car while sliding John across the leather upholstery. He slid John over until his head was nearly in Walter's lap. As he was getting up, Billy looked Walter in the face. Walter struggled to avoid Billy's eyes. Billy peered in at his one brother's evasive demeanor and then looked back to his other brother, the baby, his youngest brother, almost certainly dead or at least on death's door and his entire body shook with fury like never before. Billy fought through the feeling and climbed back into the driver's seat. He fired up the engine and pulled a tight U-turn back up Newhall and shot left onto Ashmont Street. He whizzed through the Adams street intersection without even considering using a brake. He topped 120 miles per hour on the final stretch down Ashmont Street and slammed the brakes as he pulled the mustang left onto Dorchester Avenue. He opened it up down Dorchester Ave. until just before he reached the Carney Hospital. He pulled around back to the emergency room and hopped out of the driver's seat again almost before the car came to a stop. He flipped the chair forward and reached into the back seat to lift John up again, like a father carrying a child to bed. Billy stormed through the emergency room doors screaming for a doctor until a nurse and doctor showed up with a gurney and Billy placed John on the cot.

He continued to scream and his voice was so hoarse he sounded less like a man and more like a wounded bear. As he finally let go of John, the noise from his wailing stopped but his face continued screaming. He dropped to his knees and tears began to well up and fall from his strained red eyes. He rubbed his eyes with his large, coarse hands and leant back against a table leg and buried his head between his elbows and knees.

2 THE DELI
(30 YEARS LATER)

Every Saturday it felt like the entire city descended on the "Beale Street Deli". Whether they wanted coffee and home fries or cream of broccoli soup, they showed up in the vanload from morning to night.

Jim Carson, the Deli's owner, loved this about Saturdays. His mostly teenaged, mostly hung-over staff, on the other hand were not always so thrilled.

The deli was a landmark in the city of Quincy. It was featured as a hidden gem on the local food critic TV show several times. On the face of it however, the place wasn't much to look at. It had a large plain blue sign out front that read "Beale Street Deli", written in very subtle block capital letters. From the street it was, at best, underwhelming.

Once you walked in however, the tide turned

immediately. The counter and signs showing the menu refused to buckle to the 21st century. The interior gave off an immediate sense of nostalgia as you entered the dining room. It had a welcoming sense of familiarity, kind of like walking into your grandmother's house.

There were wall to wall windows with a prime corner view of Beale Street, perfect for people watching. The tables and chairs were old, but sturdy like they were built by a craftsman at a time before Ikea and mass-produced furniture.

Even the staff, despite the grogginess accompanied with Saturday morning hangovers, added to the appeal. They were mostly local, with local accents, and 90% of them had the same haircut. That was normal considering they all went to the same local barber. The uniforms were antiques. They wore short-sleeved, blue-striped button down shirts that were always well starched. The matching blue aprons tied around the waist wouldn't have been out of place in a 1950's diner. The look felt authentic, unlike those chain restaurants and diners modeled after that era. If you ever came across someone dressed like that around town, they could only be from one place.

The Deli however wasn't always seen in such a

welcoming light. Before Jim took it over, it was mostly considered an old fashioned, outdated sandwich joint that was well beyond its prime. What Jim pulled off was nothing short of a miracle. Basically, he turned its biggest weakness (its age) into its main selling point and the neighborhood people loved it.

3 JIM CARSON

The success of the Deli not only reinvented a local business, but also seemed to define its owner. Jim Carson became known around the neighborhood as a 'Somebody'. In a city that functioned much more like a small town, Jim had become a big deal. He probably could've run for local office and come home with the victory. That type of thing wasn't for Jim though. Sure, he was happy that his Mom was proud of him and that she got to gloat to her friends about Jim (Deli or not, Jim knew she'd probably do this anyway).

Arrogance didn't suit Jim however. No one knew that more than he did. He was proud of what he'd done with the Deli and glad it was successful, but more importantly he loved the fact that he enjoyed going to work every day. Jim was smart enough to know this was no small accomplishment. Most people would never come anywhere close to that.

Jim grew into his role as a quasi-town sweetheart, at least in the eyes of his older female clientele. Older woman or not however, Jim had a knack for endearing himself to everyone. He had an easy way about him. In a way he was a natural business man. He was always affable and approachable to his patrons and his workers. He was versatile too. He could chew the fat at a bar about the Pats or Bruins and just as likely get into a Grape's of Wrath discussion with the English teachers that came in every morning for breakfast.

In any other family, Jim would've been the golden boy. Then again, in any other family Jim wouldn't have his brother Danny to contend with. Danny's achievements cast a pretty big shadow. Some people would never shake that inherent jealousy. Jim Carson however, seemed to thrive in that situation. Maybe the shadow to Jim was more like the shade of a big tree on a hot and sunny day. That's how it seemed from the outside anyway. Maybe it wasn't the only layer of his personality, but that's how many people perceived him. To everyone, he appeared content. To those that knew him best, it was obviously more than that . . .

he was genuinely happy.

The biggest reason Jim was happy had dark curly hair and brown eyes and walked into the Deli at 12 o'clock on that Saturday. She locked eyes with Jim just as he broke from his trance and finished making fresh pots of coffee at the far end of the counter. She smiled at him. An hour late or not Jim couldn't help but smile back. She took her place in the line, which was moving very quickly since breakfast had all but finished and lunch was only just beginning.

Brendan, one of the aforementioned hung-over teenagers working the counter, saw her come in and as was his way with women said, 'You all set Alex? What can I get ya?'

'Hi Brendan, I think I want breakfast, can I get you to make me a number 1?'

Brendan stood shaking his head, 'Afraid I can't do it'

'Oh . . . why not? Even for a regular?'

'I wouldn't really call you a regular. Either way, breakfast stops at 11, so I can't do it. Jim's always on me about that.'

'Hmm,' Alex contemplated her dilemma. 'So, you must turn up the heat on the grill for lunch then? And you probably just changed the fry oil?'

'Ahh . . . no we don't. We use the left of the grill for breakfast, but we keep it the same temp for lunch to keep food warm that's done and ready to go. The friolater was changed last night . . . you know, with fish & chips on Fridays, people don't really dig on haddock flavored home fries.'

'Oh, so you're out of eggs and bacon then?' She asked seeing her angle develop.

'Um . . . no' Brendan shifted and began to look irritable, 'they're just out back, but you know, breakfast's supposed to stop at 11.'

'Well . . . what could actually happen if you give in and make me breakfast right now then . . . in all honesty?'

Brendan's irritation flared up again, but he kept it in check and said, 'What'll happen is, next thing there's a line around the corner and everyone who couldn't drag their asses out of bed will be asking me to drop some home fries and do up some eggs.'

'And you know what you tell them if that happens Brendan?' Alex said with a smile creeping onto her face, her trademark dimples suddenly emerging.

'What do I tell 'em? Brendan asked, clearly agitated as he bordered on resignation

'You tell them you're out of fucking eggs, but

21

IHOP is open down the street and they do breakfast all day'

'Alright, alright, I'll make you breakfast then, whattya want?'

Alex grinned wildly as she answered, 'Two eggs over easy with bacon, home fries and toast. That's all.'

'Kind of toast you want . . . white, wheat, dark rye or light rye?'

'Tough choice . . . I'll take . . . wheat. And Brendan?'

'Yeah whatsup?' he asked as he turned to tuck the breakfast slip above the grill and reach for the bacon.

'You're very cute you know that?'

'Hands off lady, you're probably my mother's age.'

Alex laughed and pretended that the comment didn't sting a little. She walked down the counter to where Jim was standing shaking his head at her. He had witnessed the encounter with utter amusement.

'Morning Jimmy' she said brightly.

'Morning Alex, although technically its afternoon. By the way, breakfast stops at 11.'

'Anything for me though right?' She asked and winked her right eye.

Jim shook his head again, 'Guess so . . . doesn't seem to matter anyway. Poor Brendan, you turned his brain into a pretzel.'

'Oh well, wouldn't have been so easy maybe if he could've kept to a curfew last night.'

'True, true, but hungover or not, he's the best I've got, especially on a day like today. Good help is hard to find, you know that.'

'I've heard . . . so can you join me for breakfast or will you leave this damsel in distress?'

'Afraid I can't. I'm catering a funeral over on Fenno Street for some local patriarch. I have to deliver and setup shortly.'

'Ohhh' Alex pouted and pretended to be upset. 'How about tonight . . . wait, I forgot, plans to meet your brother right? The mysterious Danny Carson, so mysterious in fact, that I've never been introduced.'

Jim smiled, 'Mysterious huh? Not sure about that.'

'So why hide him then? Ashamed of me?'

'Well . . . I didn't want to say it . . . but . . . '

'Please, like anyone would believe that. Seriously though, he's your brother and he's important to you so I'd love to meet him.'

'I know. Listen, he's here for a week I think. Maybe tomorrow or Monday night? I'll confirm once I talk to him.'

Alex smiled genuinely and reached for her coffee.

'I'm free every evening this week, so looking forward to it.'

She snuck in for a quick kiss on Jim's cheek and turned to go to the table. She glanced back and through the curly locks dangling over her eyes, Jim saw her wink at him again leaving him slightly blushed. The redness was not so much embarrassment. It was more like elation.

4 MIKE RIORDAN

After work Jim ran home to shower and change his clothes. He rushed to turn around quickly. Less than an hour later, he went to meet his cousin Mike at a bar in Quincy Center.

As Jim waited for Mike Riordan to come back from his third visit to the men's room in two hours he watched Sportscenter highlights on the flat screen TV tucked behind the bar surrounded by the bottles of Smirnoff and Jameson.

The Red Sox were having a shitty start to the year, but it was still early on. 'May is no time to get into the baseball season, especially when the Bruins were still in the playoffs. Wait until mid-July', Jim thought, 'then maybe I'll give a shit about the over-paid, underperforming Sox.'

The bar and restaurant had filled up in the last hour or so. It was locals mostly on Saturdays, unlike Friday evenings. Friday's were mainly the after work crowd from the corporate offices scattered around the city. 'The Sports Bar' made a name for itself with a tastefully decorated Boston Sports theme interior and menu, which also included the signature appetizer, buffalo chicken nachos. They were not from Buffalo and barely chicken, but they were damned delicious. The bar offered a slightly more sophisticated drinking establishment for those living here, but not considered locals and also for locals living here but no longer interested in fist fighting.

Jim marveled at the bartender's perfect pouring technique and motioned to him for two more Sam Adams just as Mike came back from the men's room.

Mike was chuckling to himself as he waddled over avoiding the ping-pong ball-like movements of the wait-staff and made his way back over to the stools.

'What's wrong with you?' Jim asked confused

'Nothing wrong, just wishing they'd hang up more than just today's back page of the Herald. I had it read before wrapping up my second piss. At this stage I'm getting sick of staring at Zdeno Chara in action.'

Jim nodded in agreement, 'I hear ya, good

defenseman and all, but not much to look at really.'

'Exactly, so you're with me on this?'

'Oh yeah Mike I'm with you. They should really cater more for those with the acorn sized bladders.'

'Easy buddy, you know what holding it in does to ya. Plus, it's more likely the grapefruit sized prostate that's the issue, in fairness. Anyway, you order two more?'

'Yeah, Fast Dunny's working on it now'

'Who the fuck is Fast Dunny?'

'The dude in the short sleeve button-up behind the sticks pouring your pint'

'That fat bastard? Doesn't look that quick to me. Why they call him that?'

'Don't know man, ask him.'

Mike raised his voice so the bartender could hear him, 'Excuse me, bar man, why do they call you Fast Dunny?'

The bartender gave him a look like he complimented him on a nice watch while shoulder to shoulder in the men's room. 'Hey, go fuck yourself champ, I guess you don't want this beer after all.'

Mike, taken aback by the bartender's fervor, apologized, 'Woah, hey sorry buddy, I . . . ah didn't mean to offend . . . how much for the round?'

The bartender regained his composure and rang up the beers at the register, '$11.60'

Mike handed him $15, 'Keep it man, no hard feelings.'

In the meantime Jim was breaking his ass laughing at Mike's altercation. 'So you wanna know?'

'Wanna know what?' Mike asked, feeling irritated at the bartender's outburst.

'Why they call him Fast Dunny'

'Yeah, sure then, what the fuck, why?'

'He's got a wooden leg man . . . it's one of those ironic nicknames . . . he's not that fond of it either. You probably gathered as much.'

'Hmm' Mike murmured and tapped his index finger over his lips, 'Figures'

Jim scrunched together his eyebrows in confusion and asked, 'What figures?'

'Well, when he said 12 bucks for the two beers, I thought to myself, "What a fucking pirate" . . . so . . . it figures that he's just an eye patch and a sword away.'

Jim shook his head in disbelief over Mike's logic, 'You're fucked man'

Mike grinned extremely pleased with himself, 'Hey you brought it up asshole'

'Yeah, yeah, I know. Hey you want to know the

funny thing?'

'What else man, come on?'

'His name's not even fucking Dunny. I think it's Sheehan or something.'

Mike laughed again, harder this time, 'Why the fuck do they call him Dunny?'

'Pfff' Jim puffed his cheeks and blew air out, 'No frigin idea man.'

Jim loved this about Mike Riordan. They could just spend hours together with brains shut off just shooting the breeze about anything and nothing all at once. He found it to be the perfect escape. Not that he was escaping anything really, but with the business and pressures of everyday life, everyone needs an outlet. Otherwise they'd go crazy. Jim knew this, and catching up with Mike was one of his favorite past-times. It had been for as long as he could remember. They are first cousins, but not first cousins in that "See you on Christmas way". It was more like they were friends, same age, same town, same schools. They were close. They were pretty much like brothers minus all the animosity that comes with sharing a bedroom growing up.

Also, Jim was for Mike what Mike was for Jim, an outlet from the grind. Mike acted funny and sometimes not all there mentally, but in reality he was plenty there. He had a job that he went to each day, which was nothing to sneeze at nowadays, especially in the building industry. He also had a family, a wife and two young daughters. He had his priorities straight that was certain. His girls came first and foremost. Everything else was at least a mile away. Even meeting Jim on Saturday night was really only a favor. It was just to keep him company until his brother Danny blessed him with his presence.

'So when's Danny flying in anyhow Jimmy?'

'Actually, he flew in yesterday as far as I know.'

'Oh . . . really'

'Yeah, he had a business meeting or something yesterday evening. Then he went straight to Mom's this morning.'

'Ahh well, gotta prioritize man.' Mike took a sip from his beer, then put it back on the wet coaster and began tapping the glass with his wedding ring finger. 'Business meeting huh? So Danny's still a big shot then? Even back in Boston?'

Jim shrugged, 'Don't think big shot is the right phrase. He's a smart dude with some drive to him that's all. I doubt he'd sell his soul enough to be considered big-time in the corporate world.'

'Fuck that man, people like those hard-nose, straight talking types.'

'On paper sure maybe they do' Jim said 'but not in the real corporate world. It's all perception. People say they want someone to stand up and speak his mind. But that's all bullshit as soon as what you say and what the bosses want to hear don't quite reconcile.'

'Spoken like a jaded man Jimbo. Guess that's why you're back flipping burgers.'

Jim clearly lightened up at that comment and laughed, 'You got me pegged Mike, that's me alright, best burger flipper in Quincy.'

5 DANNY CARSON

Danny Carson took his Father's antics very personally. Growing up, anytime his Father fell off the wagon or disappeared for periods of time without notice became permanent scars on his memory. Every time Danny lay awake at night listening to the old man yelling violently at his mother it pushed him closer to his boiling point. Even today he knew his impatience and his quick temper with people could be traced back to those experiences. It was like inside he was permanently waiting for his father to come home from the corner store, which as a kid, Danny never understood why it took so long. The corner store was less than 5 minutes away on foot. There were also those times they'd be locked in the car outside some run down houses in Roxbury. Danny had to struggle to keep Jim from freaking out and running out of the car. The nerves had stuck with him. He bit his fingernails down to the cuticle still to this day.

Danny never used those experiences as an excuse however. Too many people get into some bad times and blame it all on their childhood. To blame his father for his own shortcomings, he thought, 'No way, because that's exactly what the old man would do.'

Danny did however use that fire inside him to drive himself forward. He was like the prototype of what authors for those books about children of alcoholics call the 'overachiever'. It didn't matter in what; school, sports, social activities, anything. Danny always went hard after it.

He was never really the best at any one thing, but he was never bad at anything either. Plus he was always out-hustling everyone. In sports, he played hockey and baseball. He wasn't great, but he always tried harder than everyone.

Sports were fun for Danny, but they weren't what he was working for. It was academics where he really thrived. Whether it was words or numbers, he always just seemed to get it. He also relished in the fact that he got it. He grew to love being the smartest guy in the room. That was his strength, but also probably his weakness.

To some people, Danny was perceived as cocky, even arrogant. This probably led to most of his coming of age fist fights. His stubbornness didn't help either.

He had a softer side also, it just didn't show up as often and it didn't show to everyone. His teachers loved him, his mother did, Jim, his friends and of course his wife. He probably figured that was enough and everyone else could just deal with it.

He was pretty smooth though despite this. He always had some angle. Things weren't always as they appeared with Danny. It was just his mind, always in overdrive, rounding third when you thought he'd slide into second.

That sharpness is also what made him successful. He got his MBA at Boston College and took a job in management consulting in London right after graduation. He jumped even further into the corporate world when he impressed the right client and landed in a key management position for a large multinational's European headquarters in Dublin.

No one from home knew exactly what he did, so he mainly just told people that he's in finance, which is about as vague as he can get. He preferred not to talk about work when he's home really anyway . . . well except for talking about his travels, which he always found himself doing. He preferred to come home and hear how everyone else was doing. That was just one reason of many that his first stop was always a visit to his Mother. She usually kept him well briefed on the comings and goings of the neighborhood, or as he called it, 'Who's doing who and who's getting fat.' The problem was, once he was there, she'd never let him leave.

In fact, it was his Mother's unwillingness to share him that kept him late to meet his brother at the agreed upon time, which was 8 o'clock. Instead, it was closer to 9:30 when Danny finally walked into The Sports Bar and found Jim laughing at Mike, who was making an exaggerated gesture of a cook flipping burgers with a spatula.

He pushed his way through a group of sunstroked men with beer belly's sticking out through their pastel polo shirts. As he approached he caught Jim's eye and gave him a wide grin, 'I know I'm late, but it's a bit early for charades don't you think Mike? Let me guess though, it's your wife trying to cook?'

Mikes turned and smiled when he saw Danny and laughed, 'Fuck that' he put his hand to his head like he was making a phone call, 'this is my wife trying to cook'.

Danny and Mike gave each other the guy half-hug half-handshake. He did the same for Jim only followed by a quick slap on the back of the head. 'Good to see you boys, how far ahead are you?'

'About 3 and a half' Jim answered, 'what're ya having?'

'Sam Adams . . . draught and the real one, not that nasty summer ale'

Jim nodded to the bartender and tapped his glass and gave him a three sign.

'So, Sam Adams?' Mike asked, 'I would've thought you'd be hooked on the Guinness now living over there.'

'When in Rome Mike . . . Plus, it tastes much better there. Ask any older Irish guy and he'll tell you Guinness doesn't travel well.'

'What the hell's that mean?'

'No idea, just something they all seem to agree on. How about this, 'What's for you won't pass you. That's a saying all the mother's seem to agree on.' Danny then turned and accepted the beer from the bartender's hand and nodded in thanks.

Jim laughed, 'Sounds too optimistic to be Irish,

they must've stolen that from the Chinese or something.' He took his beer from the bartender also and handed him an empty glass. 'So Dan, what's Ma up to?'

'Nothing much I guess. She was just telling me about her new job and everything. She said she's back in a clinic so she's happier.'

'Yeah, she told me that, she likes it better, at least the doctors don't treat the nurses like shit in the clinics.'

'She said that too. I have half a mind to go stutter-step some of those jerk-off doctors. Some of them with a God complex need to come down a notch.' Danny finished his statement with a healthy gulp from his pint.

Mike laughed, 'God complex huh? Man all you educated types have ego's bigger than your dicks. I bet you both spend most of your day bossing us regular folk around.'

Jim turned to Mike with a raised eyebrow, 'Ah, regular folk, huh Mike? Last I heard you've been throwing your weight around too champ. Aren't you the foreman on that Neponset bridge project?' Jim asked rhetorically.

'Hey, if I'm wearing a tool belt, I'm still regular

folk.' Mike considered his own logic for a second and took a sip from his beer. 'Who am I kidding, I don't wear a fucking tool belt anymore, I just walk around with a clip board and a tape measure . . . oh well, looks like we're all assholes then, must be genetic. Fuck them if they can't take a joke.'

Danny laughed and shook his head, 'Hey, you know something? Every time I come home I spend so much time around this neighborhood catching up and I never make it into the city. Can I interest you fellas in hitting the town for a few? Nothing crazy, I just feel like something different.' Mike and Jim looked at each first and shrugged. Both then nodded to Danny in agreement.

'Plus' Danny added, 'I think the bartender keeps shooting dirty looks over at me.'

Jim and Mike looked at each and laughed.

'Yeah Danny, what'd you say to him anyway?' Mike asked.

'Hell if I know' Danny answered, 'but I think it has to do with his limp.'

6 THE TAXI

Jim had the bartender close the tab and he insisted on picking up the bill for the last few rounds. He also insisted the bartender call them a taxi. 'Drinking and driving isn't nearly as taboo as it should be', but Jim figured 'no point in taking needless chances'. The taxi picked them up twenty minutes later outside the bar in Quincy Center. Danny asked the taxi driver to take Quincy Shore Drive so he could cruise down by Wollaston Beach. It wasn't too late and it was a warm spring night so along the beach front was still pretty busy. There were couples out still walking dogs and some small gatherings of high school kids across from Tony's Clam shop holding onto fast-melting ice cream cones. They drove past the Beachcomber, which had the bar doors open for those people smoking on the patio out front. All along the street you could hear the music playing. It was a local band, The Junkyard Dogs blasting out a Fogarty tune.

It must've been a lucky night because they hit a string of green lights starting with the Squantum intersection and all the way over the Neponset River Bridge. That meant they were on 93 North in about 2 minutes. When they hit the highway, Where the Streets Have No Name came on the radio. Mike motioned for the cab driver to turn it up. Jim rolled the window all the way down and let the warm breeze hit him in the face. 'What a night' he thought, as he sucked in the familiar Boston Harbor air. The sun had gone down an hour ago, so the city up ahead was lit up brightly. Jim looked over at the two guys and all three were smiling. Jim knew, they were all thinking the same thing; nostalgic all of a sudden for simpler times. Laughing, with friends, heading into the city, without a care in the world 'At least that's how it seemed in retrospect'. It was safe to say they all missed those days sometimes. Although they all knew those care-free times were well and truly behind them.

The view and the smell of the sea brought Jim back to his early twenties, leaving the Blarney Stone in Dorchester before going to close out the night at JJ's on Kingston Street. 'Yeah' Jim thought, 'We all missed those nights'. However, he knew memories like that often came shaded through rose-tinted glasses. He knew it was a passing feeling, but nonetheless, it was nice while it lasted.

7 THE WATERFRONT

The taxi dropped them close to Boston's North
End. They walked over to the bars on the waterfront.
The city had a good buzz about it, especially
considering it was not quite summer. They grabbed a
table on the patio of one of the bars overlooking the
harbor. The atmosphere was perfect. It was steady,
but not so packed and loud that they would get bored
staring at each other or struggle to get served. An
attractive young waitress took their order and within a
minute there were three 18 year old Jameson's on the
table. The whiskey was Danny's idea, but he regretted
it immediately when Mike took his down in one shot
and said, 'Should of ordered a few beers to go with
that Danny boy.' Jim just snickered because he knew
Danny was not impressed. He signaled for three beers

from the waitress.

Danny turned to Mike and said, 'I would've Mike, if we got Jagerbombs or Sambuca you asshole. That's good whiskey, you're supposed to enjoy the taste not suck it up like a wet-dry vac.'

'My bad Danny, I didn't realize booze came with instructions.'

'Alright, alright' Jim said, 'Enough bitching already, beers are on the way.' He turned to Danny and said, 'Hey Dan tell me about that trip to Israel for work. What's it like there?'

Danny stopped his lingering glare towards Mike and shifted towards Jim, happy to have a change in subject. 'It was strange actually. Tel Aviv's a really nice city I thought, great weather, a lot of young people, good bars, nice restaurants. I even went to a pretty sweet brew house. They have this Israeli ale called Dancing Camel, if you ever come across it, give it a whack . . . delicious. The only problem was that the whole time I always had in the back of my head where I was . . . I mean geographically. So that made it kind of tough to relax. I guess if you're born there, you're just used to that.'

'Weather was good huh . . . fucking wicked hot there I bet?' Mike asked

'Not really actually, probably 70's, really nice, it wasn't summertime though, so not sure how it gets around then. It was pretty sweet though, the hotel was along this promenade on the beach, so I jogged along the Mediterranean every evening. It was beautiful. Only one problem . . . the cats man. There were stray cats all along the promenade, and these fuckers looked way too big and well fed for stray cats, so you know they were dangerous.'

Mike gave Danny a confused look, 'What the hell are you talking about cats for?'

Jim started to laugh and turned to Mike 'Did you forget Mike, Dan here has somewhat of a feline phobia. He's had it forever.'

'Not forever' Danny corrected, 'Only since that crazy asshole down the street opened the door for us trick-or-treaters with a mutant cat in his kitchen. It had a cat face and was about the size of a St. Bernard.'

'Yeah boys, sorry, but I'm fucking lost' Mike said while scratching his head.

'Let's just say Danny hasn't been the same since' Jim added, 'Nearly every creative writing essay in school since was cat-related.'

Danny winced, 'I actually don't even want to talk about it anymore.'

Mike made a face like he understood, 'Okay I get it, kind of like Batman and bats, only without all the cool shit, like crime fighting and the Bat Mobile. Anyway, you make it to Jerusalem?'

Danny's eyes twitched suddenly with excitement, 'Oh, yeah, what an incredible place. I've never seen anything like it. You can't help but get caught up in the history, everything's so ancient. To actually stand on the ground where Jesus Christ himself stood, it's a pretty special feeling. I don't know man, just to look at the city and consider how much blood's been spilt in the last two thousand years over pretty much a claim to this place. It was wild.'

'Yeah, and the kicker is' Mike said, 'You got three religions battling over it and they're all probably talking about the same frigin God.'

Jim looked surprised and asked 'When the hell did you get so political Mike?'

'Was laid off during the winter Jim, I was hooked on the History Channel and Discovery HD. That's some compelling shit.'

'What is?'

'Fucking history man'

'Pretty ambiguous there Mike, but I get your point.' Jim turned back to Danny, 'I heard you brought Ma back some cross Dan.'

'Yeah, a Jerusalem cross. It's one big cross in the center and four smaller crosses surrounding it.'

'What's it mean?'

'I'm not 100% positive, but I do know it's supposed to represent Christianity as a whole, meaning all sects, not limited to just Catholic or Orthodox or whatever. I think it's based on some of the Crusaders' crosses, maybe the knights from Malta, but I'm not sure.'

'Sounds like something right up her alley anyway, I bet she loved it'

'Hope so . . . hey, I almost forgot.' Danny dug into his pocket and pulled out a tiny wooden case and handed it to Jim, 'I got you something too Jimmy. Happy early 30th, I figured I might not be able to come home for it, so I picked this up in Jerusalem too.'

'Thanks Dan, you didn't have to do that.' Jim rubbed his hand over the smooth wooden case and noticed the almost silky feel to it. He held it up to the lantern to look at it in light and noticed the slight grains and color changes throughout.

'Hang onto that case too actually, it's hand-carved olive wood, but go ahead open it up.'

Jim put the case back on the table and opened it. Inside there were two shining cufflinks that look like ancient coins, rimmed with gold and gold fasteners.

'They're ancient Roman Empire coins. I remember you used to be big into Julius Caesar and the Romans. They're authentic, at least they better be, because that's what the guy who sold them to me said. Anyway, I thought you might like them.'

'Are you kidding me, I love them Danny, thanks bro' Jim got up and gave Danny a bear hug.

Meanwhile the waitress came back balancing a tray with three beers on it, 'Sorry for the wait fellas, I would've put a rush on it if I knew you'd get so emotional over it.'

Mike called the waitress around to his side of the table to pay. He winced as reached into his pocket. His hands, like a lot of builders, were tough and calloused, but also dry and riddled with tiny cuts from vigorous hand-washing. He pulled out a worn leather wallet that was speckled with paint and stucco. He found a twenty inside, pulled it out and handed it to the waitress. 'It's just a brotherly love moment, that's all. Feel free to stick around and talk to me, I'm feeling left out.'

'Love to, but I've got other tables' she went to

hand Mike the change, but Mike waved it away. 'For your trouble hon, for your trouble.'

8 CARSON BROTHERS

They finished another couple rounds of drinks before the breeze picked up off the harbor and it grew too cold to sit outside on the patio. They decided that was their cue to leave and got the waitress to call a taxi.

The taxi dropped Jim and Danny off at Jim's apartment on Adams Street across from the Cedar Grove cemetery. They split the taxi fare and prepaid for Mike to get back to Braintree. It was the least they could do considering they made him abandon his truck in Quincy.

It was quiet on Adams Street, which made sense since Jim's neighbors, for the most part, were one leafy park, a little league baseball field and a few thousand corpses resting across the street.

Jim moved to this two-family house in the last couple of months. Since he moved in, the place had really grown on him. He liked it much better than his old bachelor pad over at the renovated chocolate factory. This place had three bedrooms, a kitchen, dining room, big living room and even a spacious entrance hall. It also had a front porch overlooking Adams Street and the cemetery grounds.

Jim showed Danny the spare bedroom and gave him the tour of the rest of the apartment. He lent him an old Suffolk University hoodie to throw on and they sat out on the front porch for a nightcap.

'Big place you got here Jimmy. How's about you tell me now why you got three bedrooms? You holding something back?'

'You're always observant Dan, I'll give you that. Don't read too much into it though' Jim said. Jim was glad it was dark, as he knew his cheeks started to blush at the question.

'Good, I hope I would've heard something about it at least. Seriously though, Ma mentioned your girlfriend. Alex right? Getting pretty serious I gather?'

'You could say that. Still can't believe you've never met her though. She's moving in man, end of the month as soon as her lease is up on her current place.

Half the shit here is actually hers.'

'Haha' Danny laughed, 'I was gonna ask about the throw pillows alright. I thought that was a bit strange for a grown man living on his own.'

'Nah, that's her. I stick to pillows people can actually use.'

Jim reached down and popped the top off two bottles of beer at his feet and handed one to Danny.

'There's more too Danny . . . I bought her a ring. I haven't given it to her yet or anything though. Her father's kind of old fashioned so I want to go and ask him first.'

'Jesus man, that's great news' Danny threw his hand on Jim's shoulder and gave it a squeeze 'Congrats Jim.'

'Don't congratulate me yet bro, wait until she says yes first.'

They talked for a while more after that. Jim told Danny more about Alex. He talked about how they met at the deli when Jim first worked there years ago when her uncle owned it. And how her family had moved to the U.S. from Romania when she was about 8, but she has no trace of an accent. He told him how she had gone to private schools and never really hung around the neighborhood but was still very street savvy and down to earth.

Back when he was just a part-timer at the Deli, he had always timed it so he had waited on her whenever she came in to eat. After a while he began timing it so he could take a break and eat with her. All through college they kept in touch, but really only as friends. When Jim took over the Deli as owner she still kept coming in. By that time, she was just coming in to see him.

Danny sat and listened to every word his brother said. The more he heard him gush about this girl, the more he knew he liked her already. He liked her because she made Jim happy and even though he had a pang of jealously over it, he knew Jim deserved to be happy. Jim was always the kind of guy Danny wished he had been. Not that Danny was a bad guy, but he could never just be happy. He was never content with anything. It was part of what made him successful, but it also drove him crazy. Sitting there with Jim just hanging out, relaxing and talking, made Danny wish (and not for the first time) that he could be there more often. He wished he was there more for Jim, for his Mom, everything. Part of him knew that it was a futile feeling however, plus it was probably too late anyway, each had their own lives now.

After finishing off the beers that were in the fridge, the two brothers said their goodnights. Jim had to open the Deli in the morning and was already sacrificing a good portion of his sleep, not that he minded one bit. Danny agreed to meet Jim and Alex the next night for dinner in Quincy Center around 8:30. Danny promised to be punctual this time and even offered to pay for it if he was late, something he had planned to do anyway.

9 FLYNN MCBRIDE

Brendan Maguire was a bright kid. He made good grades in honors-classes in high school without overexerting himself. He also worked up to 25 hours a week at the Beale Street Deli. He worked there since sophomore year and also picked up more shifts during the summers.

By senior year in high school, his parents knew he and his friends were into drinking. They figured most kids were at that age. They also figured he was smart enough to be responsible. They were probably not the first parents to make that mistake. Most weekends, Brendan left his car home and headed out on foot with his friends. Usually they'd head down to Merrymount Park on Fenno Street, which had basketball and tennis courts out front and dense woods in the back. The woods were where they usually stashed the coolers of beer. They'd hang out on the courts until 10pm, when the basketball court lights went off. After that they'd head deep into the woods and continue drinking. If it was a really good weekend, someone's parents would be out or away and word would get around of a party.

It was that kind of night when Brendan and his friends headed to Dora McBride's house on a side street off of the beach. Her father was a Boston cop and more often than not he'd either be working or blowing off some steam at one of the bars in North Quincy on weekend nights. Brendan had heard that Dora's mother took off years ago and was barely heard from anymore. Reports of why she left were mostly speculation, but he heard that she left because she couldn't handle the pressure of being married to an alcoholic cop. Maybe it was the combination of the two that turned her stomach. Either way, she left one day and that was that. Dora for her part seemed older beyond her 18 years. She was kind of a bad-ass in Brendan's eyes and more than a little intimidating. She took a liking to Brendan though and they hit it off pretty well. They had begun some form of a relationship, but he wouldn't call her his girlfriend.

She always seemed to have the upper hand however and this left Brendan always trying to impress her. For a pretty smart kid, he made some bad decisions. He started dabbling in soft drugs first like smoking weed and occasionally eating mushrooms. He balked at anything harder than that like cocaine or any pills like Oxycontin and Perc 30's, which had a strangle-hold on much of his generation. He wouldn't take them himself, but eventually he did try to gain her favor by creating a supply line between the source, Dora's 25 year old brother named Flynn and the end user, Brendan's buddies.

Flynn was like many misguided, under-educated men in Boston. He had a quick temper and faster hands. He made a name for himself as a teenager in the Golden Gloves boxing tournament. Unfortunately for the community, the local trainer in the boxing gym wasn't a great person to have influencing their children. He was connected with big-time drug dealers from South Boston. He lived to recruit the city's impressionable young tough guys into his ranks. He trained fighters and often times he turned fighters into enforcers. He gave them some small cash, which they had never seen before, and promised more if they could deliver results.

Flynn turned out to be the cream of this crop. Also, Flynn's old man was a cop, so he availed of some additional protection, at least while he was a minor. No cop wanted to be responsible for putting another's kid into juvenile hall.

Flynn played this card as often as he needed. He felt he deserved any leniency thrown his way. Therefore, he had pretty much run amuck and did whatever he pleased from about the age of 15.

When he met Brendan, he didn't mind one bit that he was doing whatever with his sister. He felt so unthreatened by him he almost pitied him because of how out of his depth he was in dealing with Dora. He wasn't one to leave the exploitation of individuals to amateurs however, so when he saw the grip that Dora had on this kid, he saw opportunity knocking.

Of course Brendan and his boys wanted to get in tight with Flynn McBride. That was like instant street-credit to middle class white boys. So Brendan started introducing people he knew that were looking to score to Flynn. After a while, Flynn no longer wanted to deal face to face with these newbies, so Brendan started working as an intermediary. He'd bring cash to Flynn for whatever was available. For Brendan's friends and acquaintances it was mainly pills, downers like OC's and Percs that they wanted.

Somehow that stuff started out as less offensive and taboo than cocaine. Unfortunately for many, it was also the first step towards sticking a spike your arm.

As Brendan became known more and more among his peers as someone who could supply anything, his confidence started to increase. It grew to the point that eventually he had the balls to ask Flynn to front him some product. Flynn agreed. All he could see was dollar signs those days. Most of those dollars were finding their way immediately up his nose, so his decision-making ability was more impaired than usual.

He should have known that Brendan didn't have the muscle to keep an eye on his merchandise or even make an attempt to protect it.

'He basically served it on a platter to those Mattapan brothers and they even felt bad for him and barely even roughed him up for it. What the fuck was that retard doing on the Milton Street trolley anyway? He's from fucking Wollaston Hill?' Flynn screamed at Dora when she gave him the news. 'How much is he fucking down?'

'Twenty-five hundred he said' Dora replied.

'Well tell that fucking chicken-shit he owes me five

grand. There's a mark-up for making me look fucking weak.'

10 DORA'S HOUSE

Brendan knew he had to go to Dora's party on that Saturday night. He also knew he had to have some kind of plan for getting Flynn's money back. So, when the Deli closed up shop in the evening, he said goodbye to Jim, but not before he pilfered the spare set of keys to the Deli's office. Brendan knew that if it was busy and they closed late, that Jim wouldn't have time to make it into the bank to deposit the day's take. When that happened, Jim had to either take the cash home with him or drop it into the safe downstairs.

Brendan figured there'd be at least five grand in there from a Saturday, especially one that was so busy. All he had to do was give Flynn the keys and explain the operation. Go in, middle of the night, pop the lock on the safe, grab the cash and head out. It was such an old building, that there were no cameras inside. Jim was waiting until after spring to get them installed. As far as the alarm was concerned, Brendan knew the code. He had watched Jim punch it in about a hundred times.

Brendan and a few friends got to Dora's house just after 11pm on Saturday night. They had hung out drinking beers in a friend's mother's basement and playing cards for most of the evening. Brendan wasn't very vocal about his current predicament, but his friends knew something was troubling him. They played a few hands of poker early, but Brendan just kept folding before the flop.

He didn't even argue when someone put the TV show Cops on, which was the first time in his life that Brendan didn't complain about having to sit through that garbage. The boys were pretty clued in however in the type of business that Brendan was into. It was Stevie Black, one of his buddies who he went to meet in Dorchester that day. Stevie worked at a pizza shop in Dorchester and had an aunt on River Street. It was her house he and Brendan were headed to so they could try and get a ride home when they got jumped. Since then, word had spread that Brendan was in a jam with Flynn McBride. However, Brendan would never tell them what his plan was. Half those guys had worked for Jim before and the other half were regular customers.

The door was unlocked as usual at Dora's, so Brendan knocked, trying to keep his hand from trembling. 'Hello . . . Dora?' He said tentatively and walked in. The kitchen was on the left, it was outdated with old wooden cabinets and 1970's wallpaper. A clock and a couple of wooden utensils hung on the walls from hooks and looked like if taken down, you'd still see the outline.

Brendan saw empty Bud Light cans upside down in the sink and a pizza box on top of the stove. He heard music coming from the back porch and could smell the familiar mix of cigarette smoke and marijuana drifting from the open windows.

Dora called up from the basement, which was set up as a lounge with a makeshift bar, a couple of couches and a really nice, really out of place pool table. Brendan looked back at his friend and motioned for him to bring everyone downstairs to Dora. That's where they usually hung out anyway. He said he'd be a minute and continued through the hallway to the back porch. He knocked and opened the screen door to the porch.

Flynn and his side-kick named Mike Faye both stopped talking and looked up when they heard the screen door squeak open and saw Brendan walk through it. They were both sitting in what looked like old, splinter-ridden Adirondack chairs. Flynn was holding a half smoked joint and his eyes were glazed over. His hair was buzzed down to about a 3-blade and he was sporting what looked like a chin strap, roughly about the same length as his hair. He had on a pair of baggy jeans with flip flops and an old ratty t-shirt. He looked like he was on the final stages of a bender. 'It's strange' Brendan thought 'I've never seen him so mellow looking.' That changed as soon as Flynn spoke.

'What the fuck are you looking at, you fucking coward? You have my fucking money or should I let Dozen here chew your fucking fingers off?'

Dozen was Mike Faye's nickname. Although only very few people called him that. Rumor was, he was a fat bastard of a kid growing up and could always be found in Dunkin Donuts ankle deep in Boston cream donuts. So naturally, Dunkin Donuts became Donut, which became Donuts, plural, which became Dozen. After his heroin problem really got off the ground though he got so skinny it became more like one of those ironic nicknames. Either way, Brendan called him Mike, for fear of getting cut up, or worse.

'I was hoping I could talk to you a minute Flynn, about what I owe you?'

'So . . . talk mothafucka, I'm already losing interest and think I might let the big dog loose on ya' he said and pointed over at Dozen with the joint between his index and middle fingers.

'I was hoping I could talk to you in private. I have an idea on how to get your cash back.'

Flynn leaned forward and put his elbows to his knees. He took a drag from his joint and holding the smoke in his lungs he said, 'You got something to say to me, say it now. No secrets between me and Dozen.' Dozen nodded in agreement.

Brendan shrugged slightly and considered this. He figured he had no choice but to let Dozen in on the plan too. 'I work at a Deli, you know that right?'

'You gonna pay him back in fucking pastrami, dip shit?' Dozen asked, pleased with his quick wit.

'I took the keys tonight, and . . . I think there's at least a few grand in the office safe.'

Flynn leaned back again in his chair, 'So why the fuck are you standing here! Go get it and fucking bring it to me.'

Brendan shifted his feet at the sound of Flynn's raised voice again. He dug his hands in his pockets and continued. 'It's not that simple if I don't want to get caught. If I use the keys to get in and clean the place out he'll definitely know it's me or at least someone who works there.' Plus, Brendan thought to himself, 'Jim probably wouldn't be insured for that.'

'Why would you getting caught be my problem?' Flynn asked.

'It's not Flynn, I know that, but if you think about it, I did funnel a good chunk of business your way. If people that know me, see me go to jail or something, they might be scared off going to you for anything.' Brendan answered.

'Well, I'll tell you what I think . . . I think that's a weak-ass excuse because the bottom line is, I don't need fucking shit from you. You think one of your fucking bed buddies wouldn't just take your place? What the fuck would I need with someone who just ups and loses my shit without a fight? Actually, now that I think of it, get your fucking faggot ass out of my house!' Flynn yelled. At the same time Flynn sprung to his feet and fired a half-full beer can towards Brendan that hit him square on the chin.

Brendan flinched to brace himself but was too

slow and stumbled back into the screen door and made it rattle, nearly knocking it off the hinges.

Brendan, while holding the newly formed cut on his chin, turned and struggled to open the door and step over the threshold. Flynn took two quick steps forward, pulled him back and slammed the door shut. 'Where the fuck do you think you're going?'

'I . . . I was leaving Flynn . . . I thought you said . . .'

'I'm up now asshole, sit down and tell me about this place, we're going tonight.'

11 THE BREAK-IN

Jim's alarm started screaming at 4:30 in the morning. He woke suddenly and forgot what he had been dreaming immediately. He reached over to the side table to grab his cellphone and turn off the alarm. He knocked over a couple of books and half a glass of water in the process.

He flicked the lamp on and sat over the side of his bed. He wasn't really hungover, but definitely more tired than usual and could certainly feel those few drinks from the night before. Jim was not a snooze button person when it came to alarms. He knew that was a slippery slope, especially when he had workers waiting out in the cold for him. He played through the pain of getting up right away and jumping into the shower. At least it was warm, which made it easier to roll out of bed. Boston winters get pretty cold and few things are enticing enough to make anyone want to venture out in the dark mornings.

Typically Jim would not do any drinking the night before an early start, but having Danny home was an occasion to celebrate. Also, working on Sundays was such a rare occurrence, he felt he could endure this one time. Generally he'd never open Sunday mornings unless some sort of event required it. That Sunday, he felt he had to open as most of his 70 plus clientele were headed to a one-month anniversary mass for one of the volunteer workers at the Clay Street Senior Citizens Center. He was a young pre-med student in Boston who volunteered every weekend at the senior center. A month ago a drunk driver ran a red light at the intersection of Newport Ave and Beale Street and hit the kid just as he crossed the street. It was a neighborhood tragedy. The funeral was held at St. Ann's Church in Quincy and there was standing room only in the church. Jim catered the gathering at the senior center afterwards for basically no money. With the early Mass on at about 6am, he promised the center's coordinators that he'd be open for breakfast afterwards.

Therefore, there he was digging around under the

bed for his other shoe. He was trying his best to keep the noise down since Danny was still sleeping in the next room, but he'd forgotten to lay out his stuff the night before. He went right from the porch with Danny to talking on the phone with Alex before he fell asleep. He gave her the good news, that they were meeting Danny later for dinner, so she'd have her chance to meet him at last. Alex was thrilled and she promised to drop by for breakfast early at the Deli before she went out to buy something to wear.

Jim left the house pretty much awake. At least he had showered, shaved and dressed by 5am, just a few minutes behind schedule.

At that hour anyway, the drive to Quincy was less than 10 minutes. With no State Street Bank traffic on a Sunday, he took Newport Ave all the way up past Wollaston Train station and took the left onto Beale Street. He pulled the car to a stop out back by the dumpster. The clock read 7 minutes past 5 when he put the car into park. He marveled at the quick timing, 'All while doing the speed limit more or less' he thought.

Jim walked around to the front, feeling the fresh morning air, which did him a world of good. It was warm, but the cool sea-breeze had hung around during the night and was still strong in the morning.

He reached the door and fumbled for a second with the keys to open the lock. He walked in and headed over to punch the code into the alarm system, but noticed it was unarmed. 'That's odd' he thought, 'I guess I did leave in a rush yesterday evening to go meet Mike and Danny.' He couldn't actually remember setting it. 'Oh well', he figured 'must've just forgotten'. He let it go and walked around to behind the counter. He turned the coffee machines on first and set a pot for brewing. It was still early enough that he could setup and enjoy a coffee at the same time. He continued over to the grill area and crouched down to turn the dials on, left side on low, right side on high. He stood up and held his hand over the back to make sure the flame had lit. 'It wouldn't be the first time the old grill's pilot went out.' When he felt the heat start to rise he nodded to himself happy to avoid a morning of repairs.

He switched on the friolater next and then checked the small refrigerator and was happy to find he remembered to have someone chop up the potatoes and onions the night before. 'That would do for the first round of home fries.' Happy that all that needed turning on was on, Jim went over to the front door again and put the keys in and locked the door up. That was always his practice whenever setting up alone and heading to the back or downstairs to the office.

Jim poured coffee into a mug and dropped in some milk and turned to walk out back to grab the till from the office. He hit the light switch on his way around the kitchen and was about to take his first step downstairs when he saw something strange in his periphery.

The back door dead bolt had been pulled open and the door was just slightly ajar. He tried to remember whether he had noticed it when walking around the front, but was drawing a blank. He took two steps back away from the stairway and the realization hit him. He felt a burning feeling in the pit of his stomach. His saliva dried up and he couldn't swallow. His blood rushed to his head and caused a sudden onset of dizziness. Then he heard something, a rustling noises from downstairs. It could only be someone looking for something in the office.

Suddenly, he heard a noise to the left of him. It came from the walk-in fridge across from the back door. His body jolted left quickly and he was a meter away from a pale and thin man carrying a case of bottled cream soda. The man froze at once, his gaunt face showing surprise.

Jim recognized the man from around the neighborhood, a known drug addict and all around scumbag.

'Oh fuck' Dozen swore and dropped the bottles crashing on the floor. He made a move for Jim, but Jim shot up with his right hand, throwing his hot coffee in Dozen's face. Dozen took a step back and yelped, going down to a knee in the process. Jim turned to run towards the front but lost his footing in the spilled soda that gathered around his shoes. He scrambled quickly to his feet and turned back around just in time to see Dozen leap again towards him. This time he was brandishing a knife. Dozen swung the knife with his right hand, stomach-height but Jim jumped back in enough time and rifled the empty coffee mug towards Dozen's head. He just missed, and Dozen recovered and thrust the knife straight towards Jim's stomach. Jim shifted his feet back quickly to avoid the cut and this time reached forward and managed to grab Dozen's forearm. The knife caught Jim in the stomach, but just slightly. In one motion, Jim slid his hands down to Dozen's wrist and twisted it so the knife turned upwards. Dozen's wrist made a popping noise and his head and chest lurched forward. Still putting pressure on the wrist, Jim let loose with a kick that hit Dozen square on the bridge of his nose. The crack echoed in the kitchen and Dozen's broken nose exploded in red immediately. Jim followed up right away with an elbow to the back of his neck and then hooked him to the ground still holding on to the knife hand. Despite the blood, Dozen still fought and Jim was on top of him trying to knock the knife free. That's when Jim felt a blow from behind. Something hard and heavy thumped him on the top of the spine and he immediately fell to the side and rolled onto his back. He could see clearly. He felt . . . not pain, but a sting and then numbness. He knew then he was done for. As he was pounded on, he shut his eyes to avoid watching the repeated blows. His mind began to flicker, flashes of Danny and Mike laughing, his Mom smiling, even his father, and then finally Alex, her face, those dark eyes, those curls, her dimples, and then it all faded and he saw nothing but black before he drifted from consciousness.

12 BRENDAN MAGUIRE

It dawned on Brendan what he had done the moment he watched Jim Carson turn the corner and let himself into the front door of the deli. He sat there frozen with fear in Flynn McBride's truck. Well . . . maybe he realized his mistake before that too. As the night turned to early morning, he watched Flynn fill himself with whiskey and red bull. Then he watched him snort the lines of cocaine off the patio table. He knew all along the type of person Flynn was, but he still served this up to him on a platter.

'Who am I kidding', Brendan thought. About a year ago, he watched Flynn jump an old homeless guy and repeatedly kick him in the face. The whole time Flynn was laughing hysterically. He knew he shouldn't have gotten into bed with this animal. Now this happened. He knew he was wrong, he just wish he'd realized sooner. He tried to back out that night. When he did, Flynn put lit cigarettes out on his arm until he handed over the keys. Then he was dragged at Dozen's knife point to the front door until he disarmed the alarm system. As soon as he saw Jim, he remembered bitching to him about having to chop potatoes and onions before he could go home. That was at work the night before. How could he forget, the memorial Mass was tomorrow for that kid who got hit and killed at the Newport and Beale intersection. Of course Jim was opening the Deli for that.

Brendan's brain was too occupied with dread when he saw Jim walk in. It couldn't send signals to his legs to move. He needed to do something fast, take some action, but nothing came to him. Or maybe too many things came to him. Finally, he knew he was fucked and he had to try and intervene. He had resigned to whatever fate lay ahead when he jumped from the truck and bolted to the front door. He nearly knocked himself out running into the door, which didn't budge. He grabbed the handle and pulled at it frantically until he saw the keys dangling from the other side. Jim had locked himself in. Brendan flicked his phone open and dialed 911 as he sprinted around the back. The call connected as he reached the back door but he dropped the phone when Flynn flung the door open and ran towards the car. 'Hurry the fuck up he yelled' as Dozen followed behind him holding his nose, with blood all over his face and shirt.

Brendan stumbled to his feet and grabbed his phone. He heard the operator and spoke quickly 'Robbery in progress right fucking now! It's at The Beale Street Deli in Quincy!' He ran through the kitchen and stopped short then. His hand dropped to his side with the operator still asking questions. He could already hear sirens getting closer and realized one of the neighbors must've already called the police. Brendan couldn't think. He thought he might be in shock, he lifted the phone again and said, 'Please, you need to send an ambulance now . . . my name's Brendan . . . Brendan Maguire.' He let the phone drop slowly from his hand. He walked forward into the kitchen and knelt beside Jim, who was laid out motionless on the floor. He knew absolutely nothing about first aid. He could plainly see that Jim was unconscious and he couldn't see his chest moving. Brendan was suddenly light headed. The dizziness made him sit back and lean against the oven that was behind him. His own breathing became difficult. He started to panic when he realized he couldn't take in a deep breath. He felt like someone was sitting on his chest. He leaned on his elbow so he was parallel with Jim, but he couldn't stomach the sight of Jim sprawled-out and lifeless. He laid down on his back and shut his eyes. Within seconds he too was lying unconscious on the ground. The only difference was that Brendan's chest was moving up and down as he was still breathing.

13 DANNY CARSON

There was a car's horn blaring in the final minutes of Danny's dream. He heard it, but didn't wake from it. A vicious pounding on the door downstairs and frantic calling of his name did wake him up however. He jumped from the bed at the sound. It took him a moment to remember where he was. It was his first time staying at Jim's new apartment and he was suffering from jet lag and a mild hangover. He pulled his jeans on quickly then ran out into the hall and down the stairs, putting his T-shirt on in the descent. Through the door, still knocking loudly was his cousin Mike.

Danny felt confused at the disturbance and dread began to set in. He undid the lock and opened the door to let Mike in. 'What the fuck Mike?' he asked with concern his is voice.

Mike was out of breath and hoarse from screaming outside. 'Get your shit Danny. Something's happened to Jim, we need to go to the hospital now.'

Danny's heart began to race and his hands were shaking. He ran to the top of the stairs and grabbed a pair of sneakers and quickly pulled the apartment door shut. He ran back down to the bottom and followed Mike out who had already gone to the truck and was starting the engine. Danny jumped in the passenger side and Mike hit the gas aggressively before Danny even had the door shut. Danny held on tightly to the side handle to keep from falling into Mike's lap.

'Jesus fucking Christ Mike, what happened? Tell me something for Christsakes.' Danny yelled.

'I don't know much so far, but I'm waiting for a call for more information. There was some kind of break in at the Deli or something man. Some guys ransacked the place and Jim got beaten . . . badly man.' Mike answered.

'Fuck. Is he okay Mike?' Danny yelled.

Mike didn't answer and didn't look over at Danny either. He just continued weaving in and out of lanes to avoid hitting cars from both lanes of traffic.

'Answer me damn it!' Danny yelled at Mike and smashed his fist hard against the dashboard.

Mike finally looked over at Danny briefly. 'It doesn't look good Danny' he said quietly, showing clear signs of shock, 'He may not make it.'

At Mike's words, Danny leant back against the passenger seat and ran his right hand through his hair. 'Fuck' he muttered to himself.

Mike continued driving, whipping precariously through morning traffic and within 10 minutes he pulled the truck up to the emergency room entrance in Quincy Medical Center.

'Go!' he yelled to Danny.

Mike didn't have to say it twice as Danny pushed the door open before the truck had stopped and jumped down to the sidewalk. He went down to one knee when he landed before hopping back to his feet and running through the automatic doors. 'Jim Carson!' he yelled at reception and they gave him directions to the surgery waiting room.

He ran over and hit the elevator button several times until the doors chimed open. The elevator was empty and he pushed the 3rd floor button for surgery. He hopped up and down waiting for the elevator to open up.

When the doors opened he ran outside into the hall. A sign on the wall pointed right towards surgery and he ran flat out until he entered a large waiting area. He slid to a stop when he saw his mother sitting down staring blankly before him. There was a very attractive young women sitting next to her with tears slowly streaming down her face. Her hands were gripping the sides of her forehead and strands of dark curly hair rested over her fingers. Danny walked over slowly towards them and said 'Mom' to get his mother's attention, but her attention on the floor didn't waver. He knelt down slowly in front of the young women and looked into her eyes. She looked at him momentarily startled. Danny thought he saw recognition in her eyes. 'Danny?' she said slowly.

He nodded 'Yes, it's Danny. You're Alex?' he asked

'Yes' she answered.

'What have you heard? Where's Jim? Is he gonna be okay?' Danny asked.

She continued looking in his eyes and Danny saw her struggling to fight back tears. 'He's gone Danny. The Doctor said . . . he's gone' she answered.

Danny dropped down to both knees. He felt sick and could feel bile building in the back of his throat. Suddenly and uncontrollably, he began to sob. Through the tears and shaking, he felt Alex's hand touch his face and then rub the back of his head. He felt on the verge of collapse until she pulled his head to her chest. Danny felt his tears soaking her shirt through to the skin, but he couldn't move.

Minutes later, he heard a set of footsteps approach behind him. He slowly pulled himself away from Alex, looking into her sad eyes as he stood slowly. He turned around to see Mike standing with his cell phone still in his hand. Mike's face was ghostly white at the realization that Jim was gone. He asked Danny 'Is he . . . ?'

Danny nodded slowly and used the back of his sleeve to wipe his eyes dry. 'What did you find out?' He asked as he walked closer to Mike.

'I know who did it and I know where he lives. His name's Flynn McBride, lives off Wollaston beach.'

'Let's go.' Danny said with finality.

Mike nodded with agreement and they both started into a jog towards the elevator. When they hit the ground floor at reception, both men picked up the pace and ran outside. Mike led Danny to the truck.

Once inside, Mike reversed out slowly from the parking spot then slowly turned onto the main street. As they left the hospital grounds, Mike stepped on the gas and sped down the hill and took a left at the bottom of the street, then a right onto Furnace Brook Parkway.

Danny could feel his hands begin shaking again uncontrollably. The sick feeling in his stomach stayed with him, but he no longer had the urge to vomit, it was now more of a burning feeling. Within minutes they approached Wollaston Beach and Mike quickly swung the truck onto Quincy Shore Drive, then almost immediately off again up a side street. He pointed at the house a hundred yards ahead.

Danny felt his blood run cold looking at the quaint front lawn that housed his brother's killer. He felt nerves build up and the shaking increase. He noticed three cruisers had already circled the house. As Mike pulled the truck to a stop, Danny watched the front door open. A young man was being escorted out of the front door by a police officer.

'That's him' Mike said.

Danny held his breath for a moment. Then he jumped out from the truck. He started walking towards the men quickly and broke into a sprint when he reached the side walk. He ran right for Flynn McBride. He had tunnel vision and could see nothing but McBride in front of him. He could sense blurry blue uniforms running towards him from multiple angles. He didn't yell anything or make any noise at all. 10 yards away from McBride he tightened his fist in preparation for the fight. He raised his arm, but as he did, he felt a stiff impact hit into his left side and immediately he fell to ground. He wrestled on the ground momentarily with the officer that tackled him until he felt many more hands pulling at his limbs. He stopped fighting and felt a number of punches from outstretched arms. He wheezed and tried furiously to take in a breath. Either the tackle or the fall had punched the wind out of his lungs. He could hear Mike in the background yelling for mercy and he felt hot tears heavy in his eyes once again as he watched the officer put McBride gently into the back of the squad car and slam the door shut.

14 THE FUNERAL

The funeral for Jim Carson was held in St. Gregory's Church in Dorchester. It was the largest Catholic Church around, which was needed since so many people had gathered. Also, it made sense to hold it there, since it was seconds from Cedar Grove cemetery. The Carson's, Jim's mother Kathleen and brother Danny marveled at the irony of it all. To think Jim enjoyed sitting out on his front porch so much, looking into the Cedar Grove cemetery. No one could have known that he'd be a permanent resident so soon. Danny was sure that Jim would've found humor in that somehow. No one else found humor in what had happened however, the circumstances that brought them together were terrible.

Instead of meeting over laughs and dinner, Danny had met Alex in the hospital waiting room. Instead of sharing stories about Jim's idiosyncrasies and how he was so laid back he was nearly falling over. Alex had comforted Danny, actually holding his head to her shoulder while a grown man sobbed after the doctors made their pronouncement. She was strong for him and for Kathleen showing the gritty exterior that comes with being a first generation daughter of immigrants well used to pain and suffering. On the inside however, she was bursting with flames. At home later that day she broke down in the shower, as if the water flow from the pipes was a signal to her body that it could release those tears she had held in restraint.

Mike Riordan gave the eulogy at the funeral at Danny's request. Mike barely held his composure throughout and every so often his voice cracked, especially when he made eye contact with his wife Elaine and saw her between his two girls, holding the youngest child's head on her lap. All three had red teary eyes. Even the pastor, Father Davis had a difficult time with the service, recalling Jim as an altar boy dropping the cross at one Sunday service and his awful timing with the bells during communion.

Danny was glad Mike could give the eulogy and he was proud of him. Mike had been much closer to Jim growing up whereas Danny felt, at best he was neglectful and at worse a bully. That, in fact, was now his biggest regret. Mike managed to make people smile during the service with his witty tales of youth. He even told the story of when he and Jim were about 13, and Mike had actually managed to finally push Jim so far to the edge, that he punched Mike in the face. The people laughed especially those that knew them best, including how resilient Jim was, but how irritating Mike could be.

Danny laughed and cried simultaneously. He looked back to gauge the crowd's reaction and stiffened with cold when he noticed his Father standing in the back of the church. He had snuck in late and didn't seem to be alone, a tall dark-looking man in a suit and tie right next to him. It was most likely his guard or some policeman. He saw the aging face of a man so familiar, hair longer than normal, slicked back, thinner than he remembered and with a goatee speckled with gray. Danny peered at him in astonishment and noticed he was not just standing with his hands neatly behind his back. He was actually cuffed. Bill Carson made eye contact with Danny and nodded his head slightly. Danny however turned abruptly back around. It'd been about ten years since he'd seen him, 'He has the audacity to show up now?' Danny thought. He had disappeared by the end of the service. Danny stood on the steps of the church afterwards, looking across Dorchester Avenue. He was looking left towards the Carney hospital and right towards Bakers' Chocolate factory, but the old man had vanished like the ghost that he was. As the people filed out of the church, they engulfed him and his mother with hugs, apologies and condolences. Danny let the memory of the ghost subside. His anger at those who had done this to Jim had now dulled any feelings of animosity towards a man that had become merely a figment of his imagination.

15 LOCK UP

Brendan never thought twice about whether he'd cooperate with the police. He felt his actions had led to this terrible event and he was willing to own up to his part. Brendan's parents got him an attorney. He didn't want one. At that point in time he didn't care about the outcome. Thankfully for him, even the first officer on scene and the detective assigned the case could see his fractured state of mind and reiterated time and again it was his right to ask for an attorney.

Ultimately Brendan and his attorney asked for very little. He volunteered to serve as a witness for the prosecution in the trials of Mike Faye and Flynn McBride. In return, Brendan was granted some leniency on his sentence and also was placed in a separate prison from McBride and Faye. It was a lower scale facility, with prisoners guilty of less severe crimes.

The State of Massachusetts got Mike Faye hooked on several charges, including unlawful entry, armed robbery, assault and battery, and eventually on murder in the second degree. He could've copped to manslaughter and had a few years lumped off his sentence, but he refused to roll over on Flynn McBride. For this, Dozen was given absolutely no leniency from Judge Walter Schuman or the State of Massachusetts. He saw 5-10 years tacked onto his 15 for murder. So, pretty much, the judge told him to get comfortable in Walpole, because he was in there for a least 20.

Flynn McBride didn't skate on all charges, just the most serious. Testimony from Brendan Maguire as eyewitness and concrete fingerprint evidence put him inside the Deli, so they got him for attempted larceny. Also, when Quincy police picked him up he was holding a small quantity of cocaine, so he was hit with a minor possession charge as well.

In the end though, no physical evidence could link him to the attack on Jim Carson. Whatever he had used, which was a meter long piece of wood, used for stirring soup, had left the deli with him. It probably ended up in a fire place. The police and investigators did what they could to make an example of Flynn, but it was fruitless. Everyone knew it was him who beat Jim Carson to death. But, no evidence or testimony from Brendan could actually directly link him to the attack, at least not beyond a reasonable doubt. All it would've taken was even the slightest cooperation from Mike Faye, however Faye took all of it on himself.

He took total responsibility for the attack and subsequent killing of Jim Carson. And so, for the death of Jim Carson, the main person responsible had walked pretty much scot-free, less than 2 years in jail. He was thrown in, a murderer, with the car boosters and petty thieves, still cocky, still bragging, and out in less than 24 months.

16 JOÃO

Brendan looked up from the letter he was writing and stretched his neck out of the bunk to look up at Joao, 'Hey J, how are you coming along with the Lonesome Dove? Great isn't it?'

Joao, kept his left thumb on his page and leaned on his elbow to look at Brendan's outstretched neck, 'Damn Brendan, this book's about a thousand pages long. You know I only got another 6 months inside God willing . . . I'll never finish that. Plus man, you know me ingles no is good.' Joao joked with a put-on accent.

'Yeah yeah, whatever bitch' Brendan replied picking up the letter from his chest and started going over the wording again. 'Everyone knows you went to private school down in Fall River. Just cause your parents gave you a name no one can pronounce, doesn't make you a Brazilian national. Also, I've seen you play soccer and you're a disgrace to your ancestors.'

'I'm Portuguese, not Brazilian man, suppose we all look alike to you?'

'Who's we then? If you're Portuguese, that's European asshole. I would've pegged you as Puerto Rican if anything.'

'Whatever you say muchacho, I am pretty damn good at baseball too. Maybe I am fucking Puerto Rican. You think my folks lied to me? Maybe I'll start calling myself Juan.'

'At least people can say that name, maybe turn Pires to Perez too while you're at it.'

'Of course bro, I'd say my father would love that.'

'You are in a cell man?' Brendan said jokingly, but regretted right after

'Hmm, good point man, guess that ship has sailed already.'

'Ahh, you know I'm playing J, your folks still love you.'

Yeah I know man, can't say I done them proud though brother.'

'You will man, just keep your nose clean after this round . . . still early, you got time to turn it around.'

'Thanks preacher boy, think you're throwing stones from the porch of your glass house there cousin.'

'Guess you're right man . . . Obrigado'

'Haha, fuck you asshole' Joao said as he lay back against the pillow and resumed from his spot in his book.

Brendan was put in a cell from the start with Joao Pires. You could call him lucky to a degree. Joao was about the same age, maybe a little older, but he was in tight pretty much with most minority groups. The place wasn't Shawshank or anything, but still tough enough that a clean cut boy from the suburbs wouldn't last long alone out on a limb. Joao and Brendan hit it off pretty quickly despite not having a great deal obviously in common. The troubled son of a Portuguese immigrant from Fall River and a middle-class college bound Irish-American from a quaint Cape Cod style bungalow didn't seem like a good match.

Their circumstances weren't that dissimilar however. Both, deep down, were good people whose moral compass hit a temporary dead zone. Both were from hard working, values driven families. Where Brendan mixed himself up with the drug scene, Joao's poison became taking things that didn't belong to him, mainly sports cars. Regardless, they both ended up in Dedham correctional facility for relatively short stints in jump suits. Joao had about 3 months in when Brendan joined him, but he knew people in the clink already. He wasn't tied in with gangs or anything, but when you grow up in tough neighborhoods you get to know tough people. So, Joao had a leg up on learning the ropes of the place and learning how to cope with life on the inside.

By the time Brendan showed up Joao had somewhat of a routine down. They were locked up for almost 17 of 24 hours, minus maybe 8 for sleep during the night, so you're looking at 9 hours give or take of pretty much nothing. Joao showed Brendan the prison workout routine, which consisted mainly of push-ups, lunges, squats, sit-ups and the plank. Brendan got Joao hooked on stories. The prison had a three-at-a-time book limit per person per cell, so Brendan would have his mother order them from Amazon and ship them in intervals. It was prohibited to give the prisoners books or anything else during a visit, so that was the easiest way. If he started getting through them too quickly, he'd have his mother address the books to Joao. He figured they're all going to the same place.

The rest of the time they were loose in general population, which consisted of rec time in the yard, jobs and eating. Brendan was surprised at first how well they were fed. It wasn't gourmet by any stretch of the imagination, but it was okay and you could get three square meals a day.

He guessed it was probably the path of least resistance for the prison and it went a long way in keeping the atmosphere cool.

It was during the general population time where Brendan's friendship with Joao, and Joao's network became so obviously important. Word was out that Brendan had given up information on McBride, so there was always a chance of someone trying to make an example of him.

During rec time, it was outside when you could see the cliques and class system develop. Many of the inmates were short to medium timers, but there were still some tough dudes walking around that would rough you up for next to nothing. 'At least there were no serial killing psycho's floating around.' Brendan thought. Still, he never quite found comfort in that thought alone.

Brendan and Joao walked outside together. It was a decent day weather-wise, a few clouds floating around, but they were puffy white ones with no threat of rain. There was a good portion of sun getting past the clouds as well, and best of all no humidity. 'Nothing worse than very hot and very humid, especially trapped with hundreds of caged convicts,' Brendan thought. 'Humidity always seems to bring out the worse in people, making even the most docile riddle with agitation.' Had he not been where he was, he'd have nearly called it pleasant.

The two boys walked through the yard past a couple of weight lifting areas. Brendan liked to work out, but he felt those dudes pumping the weights were not an approachable bunch. He figured he could stick with the Count of Monte Cristo workout at least until his time was up. He was safer that way.

He and Joao did play basketball however. Brendan was more of a hockey fan growing up, but everyone growing up where he did played at least some hoop. It was a convenience thing. There were courts everywhere and all you needed was a ball.

Brendan followed Joao over to behind one of the hoops. Joao fist bumped with a few guys stretching out under the net and asked if they could get in. The two of them made 10 in total looking to play, so they decided to run full court. They lined up at the foul line to shoot for teams, first five to hit a free throw. Joao and Brendan ended up on the same team with two Brazilian guys and an Asian guy named Nguyen. Brendan was a head taller than everyone else on the team so he won the job of center. The other team was better for size. There were two white guys, one tall and stick thin called Jason and another older guy they called McNally, who had graying, balding hair but was built like a cathedral. There was also a shorter black kid named Ray, who they all knew because he was the best on the court almost every day. The Chang twins rounded off the side. Brendan didn't really know them, but apparently they ran with some of the Chinese Mafia near Kingston Street in town and both got done for Breaking and Entering. Brendan didn't think they were really twins, since besides both being Chinese, they shared no resemblance. He wasn't sure whether they were even both named Chang or if it was a nickname.

There were no jump balls on the court. Instead of a tip off, the first to hit a 3-pointer started with the ball. Nguyen hit a 3 after Ray missed his attempt, so

Brendan kicked the ball in from under the net to Joao to start it up.

Joao took the ball up in a slow jog, letting his team set up. Ray was guarding and gave him plenty of space to start off. Joao took it over half court and caught a look from Nguyen. Joao dribbled hard right like he was driving, at the perimeter he stepped back and crossed over to his left to change direction. Ray back-pedaled and corrected, but as Joao went left Nguyen set a solid pick on Ray. Ray yelled 'switch' and McNally stepped over to guard Joao. Joao caught Brendan's move from the right side to cut in past Jason to the hoop. Joao hit Brendan with a perfect pass rifled from his left to Brendan's chest and Brendan lofted in the easy lay-up.

Joao started back pedaling on defense and fist-bumped Brendan on his way past. McNally let off a tirade of f-bombs in Jason's direction for getting beat to the inside.

McNally checked the ball in to Ray who decided to take it back hard. Ray was quick past half court and stutter-stepped Nguyen to the right, only to spin off him to the left when Nguyen went for the reach. Brendan and Joao stepped up to double on Ray, but Ray was too quick. He faked right again and Brendan bit, then he dribbled through his left leg to go left only to go behind his back, again to his right. He beat Joao with that move then hit the empty lane to the basket. Ray laid it in and ran back on defense only after some good-natured ribbing in Joao's face.

The game went back and forth at a fast pace until it was tied up at 17. With the game close and both teams wearing down, that's when each started launching 3's. Ray dribbled up the right wing, then held up for McNally to shake loose one of the Brazilian contingent on the perimeter. Ray fed him and McNally launched a 3 that fell in off the glass. Ray yelled something to McNally about being old school, but McNally was too into the game to joke at this stage.

Joao ran the ball up past half court then slowed the tempo. He was looking for Nguyen, who was scrambling, trying to get loose for a 3.

Meanwhile, Brendan tried to gain position down low on Jason for the rebound. The two had been grappling with one another all game. Jason had snuck in a several elbows to the ribs and knees to the thighs on Brendan, all the while giving him verbal jabs under his breath.

Jason kept on him. He was calling Brendan Sinatra,

saying how he'd heard Brendan loved singing to the cops. Brendan tried to keep his head about him. During the game Brendan realized, Jason was obviously one of McBride's boys or at least an acquaintance. He was wishing Joao hadn't talked him into playing basketball at all. He knew Jason was trying to goad him into something. The guy was thin, but he was lean and wiry and looked well able to scrap. Brendan thought he must be local, an older dude from Quincy maybe, but he wasn't immediately familiar.

Brendan stood his ground for the time being, and Nguyen got loose at the top of the circle. Joao fed him a bounce pass, which he fielded and fired to the basket with a quick release. The shot was just wide and clanked off the rim and back board towards the right. Brendan crouched, and then leapt for the rebound. Jason saw Brendan poise for the jump. He planted his left foot on Brendan's toes, then with a quick pivot, turned and caught Brendan's nose with his right forearm just as Brendan went for the leap. He connected cleanly and everyone on the court heard a crunch.

The crowd that had surrounded to watch the game's end now started roaring. Brendan clutched his face and went down immediately. He felt a shooting pain through the center of his brain. He tasted the bitterness of blood almost instantly and could see only blurred colors through the tears that sprung to his eyes. He heard shouts from the court and from the crowd. Some were roars of outrage, others of encouragement. Then he felt a thumping pain in his ribs and knew he was being kicked. He pulled his legs into a fetal position to try and block it, more concerned with keeping his arms over his head.

Joao had cut towards outside the key to follow his shot. He hadn't seen the initial forearm to Brendan's nose, he did hear a thump and a crack however. When he turned, he saw Brendan fall to the ground. He stopped his run to slow it down and check on Brendan. It wasn't until he saw Jason begin kicking Brendan that he realized what was going on. A crowd seemed to gather immediately and Jason kept beating on Brendan, aiming punches and kicks at areas not covered up.

Joao was quick to act. He shoved his way through the dense crowd of rowdy onlookers that had developed. He saw an older white guy grab hold of Jason and tuck something into his hand. Joao saw a flash of light from the object and it was clear right away it was a blade or at least something sharp. He managed to pick up the basketball which appeared near his feet and rifle it at Jason right as he took a swipe at Brendan's side with the blade. The ball struck Jason hard off the face in mid-swing, disrupting his attempt, although he had managed to slash Brendan's outer arm around the triceps. Jason was momentarily stunned by the hit and faltered slightly, taking a step back. A lane opened up for Joao and he ran right at Jason and tackled him to the ground.

By this time the shouts of the guards could be heard loud and clear and the crowd that had gathered to see blood was dispersing to avoid the guards' wrath. Jason was more than a head taller than Joao and had much longer legs and arms. However, Joao was pretty well built for his height, put together like a wrestler so he was showing a slight edge. He wrestled Jason to the ground trying to grab at his arm that held onto the blade. His hands were getting cut, but it appeared to only enrage him further.

Joao managed to land a couple of rights and one or two head butts, but Jason kept scrapping.

The guards finally made it through the crowd and one guard swung his baton at Joao's back and neck. He refused to stop fighting though and so did Jason.

Joao jumped up and grabbed at his eyes after another guard tried to pepper spray Jason to get him to stop fighting. Joao's arms were finally yanked free by the two guards and they pulled him off of Jason. Joao grabbed at his side as the guards pulled him away and grimaced in pain. He stopped fighting then as the two guards that held him led him away.

From the ground, Brendan looked over and noticed Joao's hands, which were covered in blood and sliced, like he had punched through a few windows. He saw the red patch growing under Joao's shirt near his abdomen.

Within just a few steps he watched as Joao's legs gave way as he stumbled forward and he passed out.

17 BRENDAN'S RECOVERY

Brendan woke hours later to a nurse changing his bandage that was wrapped around his left arm. He tried to smile at her but the nurse offered nothing in return. He tried to talk but found it too difficult to speak. His throat felt raw. He rubbed his neck with his right hand and the nurse understood his gesture.

'Throat's going to hurt for a while. Your nose is all taped up so there's no air getting through so you're breathing only through your mouth. I'll have them bring you a drink.' She finished the wrapping and taped up the gauze. She nodded to his arm and said, '25 stitches in all, clean slice luckily, but you'll probably have a scar anyway. Whatever got you was very sharp.' She finished up and turned to walk away. Before she left she said, 'There's two policemen outside the door. There's a buzzer on the table to your right. Press that if you need anything urgent. I'll see to it someone brings you something to drink.'

She left then and Brendan felt more alone than ever before. They must have given me a sedative to knock me out he thought, probably to reset the nose bone. He could feel the pain all the way through to the back of his head. He couldn't see himself but he imagined he looked rough, probably two black eyes to go with this gauzed up nose. He felt rough anyway. He felt furious too . . . with himself that is. He should have been more careful. He never should've jumped into a basketball game. It made him an easy target. 'Someone would have come at me regardless' he figured, 'so no point in dwelling on this.' If anything, having it happen so publicly was probably a blessing. At least Joao was there and had his back. He'd most likely be dead otherwise.

Once he thought that, he remembered Joao. He had no idea what happened to him. He didn't know if he was okay. He thought, 'Was he in trouble with the warden? Was he dead?' A whole new feeling of dread swept over Brendan. 'Have I sent another person to his death?' He wondered. He was sure he could not carry on any longer if so. And with this thought he clenched his eyes shut and forced all the pain towards the front of his head and let the slow tears trickle down his cheek until he dried out and there was nothing left to pour out of him.

18 RETURN TO LOCK UP

The State of Massachusetts and the warden let Brendan recover for about a week and a half in the hospital. He was still bruised and cut when he was led back into his cell by one of the guards, but still, he looked better than he had a week ago.

The bandage around his nose had been reduced to a strap and he had to see the prison nurse daily so she could change the bandages on his arm.

The doctors warned him off any sports, recreational or otherwise for the next month at least. This meant very little to Brendan anyway as he did not have the slightest intention of joining anymore pickup games. He was pretty much dead set against even going into the prison yard for rec time.

He figured he'd just wait out those hours in his cell.

During his stay in the hospital, he learned that Joao had a real close call with a stab wound to the side of his abdomen. The surgeons had worked on him pretty much immediately, which was lucky for him because there wasn't enough time to bleed out. After surgery, the doctors had kept him pretty much sedated all the time. There was some worry of infection Brendan heard, but Joao made it through pretty well.

Brendan also learned that Joao would serve out the next few months in a rehab facility, which meant Brendan would be out free before Joao made it back to finish out the remainder of his sentence. Apparently there was no disciplinary action taken against Joao as several guards testified to his involvement as self-defense. The whole thing was a relief to Brendan. He had never meant to drag Joao into his troubles, he was sure Joao had his own shit to deal with. But, knowing now that he was okay, Brendan couldn't help but feel happy that Joao was there to jump in.

By no means did Brendan feel totally comfortable that everything had blown over. He hadn't heard anything about that guy Jason, and God knows who else was floating around those jail cells on Flynn's behalf. So when the cells were open the first time for chow, Brendan entered the cafeteria filled to the brim with trepidation.

When he grabbed his tray he noticed his hands were visibly shaking. He slowly joined the line and took his turn reaching for food. Each stretch drew pain from his wounds. His eyes darted back and forth in an attempt to keep watch of his periphery in case of any sudden attacks. He decided if approached, he would first swing his tray, then try for a kick in the nuts, then run. Thankfully, he thought, no such attack ever came. At the end of the line, once he was served, he scanned the room for an area that was quiet. He headed towards the back left corner of the canteen, close to the exit doors, and found a seat at a mostly empty bench. He realized then that he was starving and couldn't remember the last thing he'd eaten. He began tucking into his plate and momentarily forgot all his worries.

As he was shoveling the last of his instant mash potatoes into his mouth, he heard the clank of a tray being put down in front of him. Brendan flinched and slid back sharply in his seat.

'Relax kid' the stranger said, if I was gonna go at

ya, you wouldn't have heard me coming.'

'That's really reassuring' Brendan thought sarcastically, but just said 'Oh'.

It took a few seconds, but a look of recognition must've swam across Brendan's face. The man noticed the look and asked, 'So you know me huh?'

Brendan tried not to nod, he didn't want to over step his boundaries. He just said, 'from the basketball game right?' I think the guys were calling you McNally.'

'That's me' the man said, 'except it's not McNally, its McNulty.'

Brendan said 'Oh, sorry, I thought I heard McNally.'

'You did' McNulty said, 'You think I tell every fucking asshole in here what my real name is?'

'No sir' Brendan answered

'That was rhetorical champ, and keep that sir shit for your grandfather.'

'Uh okay' Brendan said safely, not knowing where this was headed.

McNulty started into his food and chewed the burger beef for about thirty seconds before taking a sip of his drink and cleaning his mouth with his sleeve. 'So . . . believe it or not handsome, I'm not here to chew the fucking fat and make nice nice.'

'I figured as much' Brendan risked saying.

'You would' McNulty said raising an eyebrow, 'I heard you weren't such a dumbshit. Although truth be told, ending up in here across from me isn't what I'd call intelligent. Anyways . . . the point. I know something you might like to hear.'

'Oh' Brendan said 'Thanks'.

'Don't thank me, remember I did sit and watch you get your balls handed to you by the white Snoop Doggy Dog, figured I owe ya. To be honest, I had heard about you before. I heard that you got that Carson kid setup and left for dead . . . figured you were as good as gone. If you knew the Carsons as well as I do, Flynn McBride's recourse on your actions never would have even crossed your peanut sized mind. That fucking faggot's baby carrots compared to Carson's crew . . . especially behind fucking bars.'

Brendan visibly shrunk in his seat and muttered, 'I wouldn't have blamed them if they did . . . I never meant to . . .'

'Save it junior. I'm not your fucking priest and I'm sure as shit not your lawyer. Anyway, my story . . . I was waiting for word to come down the line to take you out. I assumed if I wasn't asked myself, I'd at least have heard through my channels. When said information never showed, naturally I became less and less interested, and before long it found its way into the 'who gives a fuck' part of my brain. It wasn't until I saw you get your roof beat in by that skinny douche bag that my interest was once again piqued.'

'Well, I'm glad my getting my ass kicked interests you.' Brendan said and immediately regretted his tone.

McNulty shot him a quick look of irritation, paused briefly, then continued. 'So, I made some inquiries into your situation. What I found out was 'A' what you already know, McBride wanted a message sent, which was obvious. And 'B', the curveball, word was out from Carson to let you go on about your business. He wanted you left alone . . . if you can believe that?'

Brendan leaned forward on his good arm showing his interest. 'Why I wonder?' He asked sincerely.

McNulty smiled, 'Same fucking thing I said. I couldn't' figure it out. So I put a few calls in. It turns out, some broad had nearly begged Carson to leave you alone.'

'Some broad?' Brendan asked. 'What girl could that be?' he thought, 'doesn't sound like Dora.'

'Some foreign broad I think.' McNulty said, 'Alex

something or other. Some Greek name maybe.'

'Alexandra' Brendan said. 'Alexandra Dumitru. It's Romanian actually.'

'What the fuck's the difference' McNulty said, 'Whatever the fuck, she saved your ass somehow. I heard she went out with the Carson kid who got killed.'

'Wow' Brendan thought, then he said, 'I can't believe that. I guess I'm lucky it was her. Jim always said she was special . . . always said she was different than other girls around here.'

'Well don't go getting emotional on me anyway.' McNulty slid back in his seat and made like he was getting up. 'You are fucking lucky ya know. Fucking horseshoe up the ass lucky, anyway kid, keep your head down and finish out your bid.' McNulty started walking away, but stopped and turned on a dime. 'Oh, and don't worry about that string bean Jason kid. Turns out he went at you because he owed McBride. He's a junky. Hit you to clear up a debt. Stupid bastard popped your Brazilian buddy though and is now going up for attempted murder. Heard a good few years are being tacked on to his sentence, so bottom line, he's no longer staying at this country club. Good news huh?' Brendan just nodded in agreement and watched McNulty turn and walk away.

After Brendan's little talk with McNulty, he felt a strange sense of relief. Over the next few days his routine, mundane as it may have been, got back in full swing and for the most part his anxieties seemed to melt away. This wasn't solely down to the information he received, although that did change him. It was more that he felt he had gotten over one big hurtle. He could now see a light at the end of the tunnel, the light being his freedom, the tunnel being the next few months.

Brendan welcomed the thought of leaving that place, but he also experienced a sickness in his gut whenever he tried to figure out what to do when he got out. Not so long ago, he thought, 'I was an aspiring college student. Maybe not headed for big things or greatness, but headed in an upward trajectory nonetheless. Now what' he pondered, 'now what is there for me?' He knew however that no one was to blame for his path and where it took him but himself. His parents hadn't raised him that way. They were great role models. They were honest, hard-working people. They were always supportive, never smothering and he had shamed them. That was his thank you to them after 18 years of love and support.

He had made them outcasts in their own town for actions he had taken alone, not them. They tried to keep their heads high and go about their lives as normal, but Brendan could see the circles under his parents' eyes on the occasions they'd visit. He saw the weight of the last year or so dragging them down, faces worn, ostracized by friends and neighbors. They had withdrawn from the community. His father, once a proud and vibrant man, now looked torn and dark to Brendan. He even struggled to make eye contact with his son when they spoke.

Brendan was sure he wasn't strong enough to go through what they had or bold enough to join them in misery, so he knew once he was out, he was gone. He didn't need to go far, but he needed to go.

With Joao still in recovery, it ended up that Brendan would serve the remainder of his sentence in his cell alone. At first it was this lonesome period that drove him crazy with unwanted introspection. After a while however, Brendan began to cherish this time alone with his thoughts and imagination. It was during this period that he began to write. For hours each day he would lay on his bunk, face first with a pillow under his chest and a notebook and pen at the ready. It started with letters. He wrote letters to everyone, not so much letters to say hello, but letters of apology. He wrote to his mother and father often. He thanked them, tried consistently to cheer them up. He wrote to the parish priest. He didn't know why really, he wasn't really religious, but he felt like at least he would likely read them. His hand broke into cramps often when he started writing initially. He hadn't hand-written anything really in years. His penmanship was atrocious and he often felt he needed to rewrite letters slowly in better hand.

Brendan felt bold in doing so, but eventually he began writing to Alexandra. He even once wrote to Mrs. Carson. He wasn't sure if they'd even read it. He thought they'd probably toss it into the fireplace without even opening it.

He wasn't sure why he did this. It wasn't forgiveness he sought, he wasn't that naïve. It was more he wanted them to know that he realized what he'd done was wrong and in no way dismissible. He did apologize, but he never once asked to be forgiven, nor did he ask for a letter in return. He never received one either. He even once wrote a letter to Danny Carson. Afterwards he thought better of sending it and ended up tearing it into a thousand pieces and flushing it down the toilet.

Eventually, he ran out of things to say in letters. It was then that he let his imagination run wild and began writing fiction. This, being inside his made-up world became like a new drug. Day and night, it's where he was, stopping only to eat and go the bathroom, and sleep occasionally. And before he knew it, Brendan was escorted from the prison with his notebooks in a plastic stop & shop bag, wearing the same clothes he did when he entered. He left the gates and walked into his mother's arms, but by this time, it had all changed and he was no longer her boy.

19 DOZEN

When Mike Faye took the wrap for Flynn McBride he thought he was the hard guy. Only a rat would roll on a buddy and Flynn was his friend. He truly believed he'd do his time and probably get paroled after 10 years. He wasn't looking forward to it or anything, but in his head it wasn't just the best option, it was his only one. Plus, he figured he would've killed that guy Carson on his own, only the bastard knew how to fight. 'Fuck him anyway' he thought, 'only a few lucky shots'.

When he first arrived in Walpole he thought he'd fit in great. Actually at first he kind of did. The first while he met a few inmates just like him. Guys that were in there because they were too tough to give in.

'Fuck 'em, give me whatever time you want Judge, I'll do that shit on a headstand.' There were plenty of young puffed out chests walking around telling each other about their escapades, telling people why they're in, how they got caught and basically running off at the mouth. Mike liked these guys. They were just like him. They were his kind of people. Gradually however Mike began to notice a lot of other types around, quieter types, dangerous looking types. He began to notice the looks from these men.

Eventually he got the feeling that maybe these were the men, and he was merely a boy amongst them. Once the initial period of settling in was over, he began to realize that maybe his pack, the guys like him, were not the right ones to emulate. He saw how these hard, stone-faced inmates looked at guys like him. They weren't respected. They weren't feared. They were a joke. That meant . . . he was a joke.

He wished he had never walked around telling people to call him Dozen. Like anyone really gave a fuck about his nickname. But it was too late, soon as his nickname went around, on came the jokes, with all types of sexual innuendo. He knew this was not the place to be associated with sexually ambiguous nick-names.

Dozen was never attacked in the shower or anything, but he couldn't help but think his time would come. He'd seen plenty of movies. He knew what happened in prison. 'That shit ain't worth taking for anybody, for Flynn or anyone else' he thought. Fortunately, but unfortunately for Dozen, no hard-man had taken a shine to him. Maybe if one had he'd have been able to protect him.

Dozen's cell was on the second story, and as the doors opened for dinner one evening he walked out of the cell and took a left to head for the stairs. Maybe if he'd noticed the lack of people in the halls or a lack of guard presence he would have turned back and skipped dinner that day . . . but he didn't. He didn't notice anything different, so he didn't turn around. He continued walking, rolling his shoulders forward in a hunch which he had developed only recently. The more confidence he lost, the further forward his head lurched when he walked.

He experienced an eerie feeling as he walked past an older man; a man with straggly looking salt & pepper hair and a matching goatee. The man was staring at him intensely, that's what Dozen noticed. Dozen dropped his eyes to avoid the gaze. He couldn't bear the man's fervent eye contact. He focused his own eyes on his feet and thought to himself, 'keep walking, don't say shit.' He even didn't react when the man brushed a shoulder against him as he walked past. Dozen tensed at the contact, but kept the same pace moving forward. He could smell the man's deodorant and feel the heat of his body temperature as they grazed shoulders. He couldn't fight the urge and after a few steps he turned to glance back at the man that had put such fear into him.

As he did this, he saw the flash of a movement close to his face and felt something like cloth around his neck. As he gasped for breath, he then felt a shove at the top of his body and something trip his feet.

As he flipped over the bars on the balcony, he saw a blur of colors which he imagined were faces. The rope wasn't long though, so his descent was brief. He felt a tug and then nothing at all.

A guard on the ground floor of the prison had entered the area just in time to hear a popping noise. He thought at first it was the sound of a light bulb bursting. But, when he looked up to check which bulb had popped, he saw a man hanging lifeless from a make shift noose crafted from a pair of prison trousers tied to the railings and what looked like a rolled up pillow case hooked around his neck. Mike

Faye died on impact from a broken neck.

20 ALEX AND JIM

Alexandra still managed to smile whenever she thought about that day with Jim when they found out Theresa was on the way, although they hadn't known whether it was a boy or girl, sor even cared at that stage.

She remembered Jim's confused look on the couch trying to enjoy his Sunday ritual of reading the newspaper and drinking coffee all day. She had told him gently what she was feeling and tried to get him to deduce the meaning. This was all in vain of course and so 'enough with the subtleties' she thought, and blurted out, 'Jim, I'm over a month late for my period. I think I might be pregnant.' He had sat there for a few seconds looking up from his paper, looking all of

12 years old with his raggy old plaid bathrobe on and huge race car slippers on his feet that he got in the Deli Christmas grab the year before.

He appeared to be thinking deeply about what to say, although it just as easily could have been his peeing in his pants look, with his brow furrowed, lips pursed and his hair still in the bedhead style he woke up with. 'Well?' Alex finally had to say to break his concentration. That's when his face finally relaxed and a broad smile gradually made its way to the surface. 'Well, if it's true' he said, 'then I couldn't be happier.' Alex saw him toss the paper aside and jump up to hug her. Her anxiety about telling him melted away in that instance.

She made him, actually, forced him to change into clothes and brush his teeth and hair before they could run to CVS to buy a test. Jim drove and he had a new found cautiousness to his driving, Alex recalled. They smiled to each other without speaking during the short drive up Adams Street to Dorchester Ave. She saw his face blush briefly when they were in the family planning section and the after-church crowd paraded into the shop. That's the Catholic upbringing she thought. He never wavered though. They had stood shoulder to shoulder in the line to pay. She could still feel the heat from his hand when he squeezed it tightly to let her know he was still excited. They paid at the counter and withstood the glances of curiosity from some people and of disapproval from others, mainly the older woman in pink outfits with crosses around their necks, and reddish freckled faces from the early spring heat wave.

The drive home again was riddled with anticipation. Not so much however as the three minute wait after peeing on the stick. Jim had insisted on pacing back and forth for the full 180 seconds, stopping only once to say, 'you washed your hands after, right?' He winked then and kept pacing.

The oven timer buzzed after what seemed like eternity. They gave each other one last encouraging look before they feasted their eyes on the results, 'Plus sign means positive, means yes we're having a baby' Alex thought to herself as Jim lifted her and kissed her.

That was two months or so before Jim was killed. She had begged him to hold off telling people until after the first few months. He had been aching to tell Danny, and they had agreed to tell him together that night for dinner. Of course that day never came and so Alex never could quite find the right time. She hated herself for asking him to keep it from his brother, but after not telling Danny at first, she couldn't bring herself to do it. Of course eventually word got out. Her parents obviously had to know as she had moved back in with them temporarily. A thousand times after Danny left she tried writing, tried to get the strength to call, but she always failed. When Theresa was born she told them all, but by that time Danny had begun his downward spiral and was barely coherent and really just lost in himself.

His apparent indifference pained her, but deep down Alex felt she was to blame. Where she found empathy was even stranger. It had begun with a letter to Mr. Carson, Jim's father. His response was kind and empathetic, not at all what she had expected from the man Jim had described. She had even paid him a visit in prison. She didn't ever ask why he was there or what he'd done, or even when he'd be out. It was good enough for her to have some connection with Jim's family. It was good enough for him to have someone to talk about Jim with. She knew the main thing they had in common was that they both thought they'd always have more time.

21 DANNY CARSON

Danny saw the email from his boss had come through at about 7:30am. He heard his phone vibrating on the table next his bed. He struggled to scrape the sleep from his eyes as he punched the pin code into the phone's touch screen. He always botched the first pin attempt in the mornings these days. He chalked it up to waning eyesight, fat thumbs and an over sensitive key pad. He noticed the time on the phone read 9:52am. The buzzing must have been a message reminder. He either slept through his alarm or heard it, turned it off and fallen back asleep all without realizing.

Danny shook his head awake and rubbed his eyes with his fingers. He slid back in his bed and propped himself against the headboard. The covers slid off him as he sat up and he felt the cold air sting his bare shoulders. The mild Irish winter had turned colder and damper than usual overnight. Danny looked to his left out of habit, expecting to see his wife Michelle sleeping soundlessly next to him. 'Must've been dreaming again' he thought. It registered that he'd been living alone in a barren one-bed apartment in Harold's Cross for a while now.

The realization dampened his mood further and once again he could barely stomach the thought of walking into that soulless glass building for work in the morning. He would have to pull himself together if he had any chance of giving the impression that he gave a damn. Although that'd be tough to pull off when walking in about two hours late.

He jumped out of bed and hustled to the closet to grab a towel. He rushed to get the shower going with hot water to melt away the coldness from the apartment. It was an old building that was not well-insulated. Plus the only heating in the place came from two space heaters, including one in the bedroom that didn't work. There was a fire place too, but Danny never remembered to buy fire logs or briquettes so it ended up releasing more heat than anything else.

After the quick shower, Danny brushed his teeth and rushed through a shave. He threw on his cleanest suit and the least-wrinkled shirt from his closet. He grabbed his three-quarter length pea coat off the hook by the door and tossed a scarf across the back of his neck as he walked through his dark hallway to the front door. He heard the heavy door slam behind him as he left and hustled down the front steps. He pulled his coat on and flicked his collar up to try and block some of the cold wind from getting to his ears. It was gray out and cold, 'but at least the rain had held off' he thought.

As he turned on to the Grand Canal towards Ranelagh he picked up his pace. He sped up to increase his body temperature not from any sense of urgency.

Danny reached Harcourt Street about 15 minutes later. He was sweating a little from the walk and he stripped off his coat after walking into the building. The receptionist gave him a knowing nod, which to Danny smacked of judgment. Danny returned only a slight eyebrow raise as he turned the corner and hit the elevator button.

He took the elevator to the sixth floor and

fumbled in his pockets for his badge to get through the hall door. He found the badge in his inside coat pocket luckily and swiped himself through to the floor. He crossed the small kitchen area and headed down the hall to his office. He always left it unlocked, 'nothing worth stealing there anyway'. He hung his coat on the hanger in the corner and switched on his laptop.

Danny decided there was no point in putting off the inevitable, so once the PC was starting up, he headed the few doors down to speak to his manager.

When he reached the office, the door was open and Danny leant his head in while he knocked on the glass. 'You wanted to see me Kevin?' he asked.

Kevin looked up from his monitor and answered, 'Yes Dan, come on in and shut the door behind you.'

Danny stepped in and shut the door behind him softly.

'Grab a chair' Kevin said and pointed with his palm open towards the chair across from his desk. Danny walked over, sat himself down slowly and folded his hands on his lap.

Kevin used the mouse to close a couple of windows on his PC then turned to face Danny as last. He took a deep breath before he started talking. 'This isn't an easy conversation to have Danny.'

Danny remained still and just waited for the punchline. He did scrunch his forehead slightly to show Kevin's words had registered. Kevin opened the drawer on the right-hand side of his desk and pulled out an envelope. It wasn't sealed, so Kevin opened it and pulled out a letter and slid it across the desk to Danny.

Danny perched himself forward and started to read through the letter without touching it.

Kevin pre-empted his response and said, 'it's not a dismissal letter Dan, but it is your final, written warning.'

Danny quickly scanned through it and looked back up at Kevin when he finished. Kevin nodded at him and said, 'It's signed by me and our Human Resources Business Manager. Technically, she's supposed to be in this meeting, but after you didn't show up at 9 this morning, she couldn't keep cancelling her other appointments all day until you decided to waltz in.

Danny gave a slight nod to indicate he understood the criticism. He said, 'The letter says there have been several complaints about me. Why is it that people can complain about me, but not to me? Where I'm from if you have an issue with someone, you bring it up to him first.'

Kevin gave a shrug and looked around his office. 'Look around you Dan. We're not on a building site in Downtown Boston here. Not everyone is comfortable with bringing their issues to your face. Besides, you haven't exactly been the most approachable person around the office here have you? People think you're liable to snap any minute.'

'Well Kevin, who are these people anyway? Who's them and they? Is it some big secret? And what are their complaints?'

'Danny!' Kevin said firmly and slapped his hand down hard on the desk. The months of leniency and aggravation started to burst through to the expression on his face. 'Forget them and they. Consider my opinion and my complaints. Consistent tardiness, numerous missed deadlines, and never mind your negative attitude and constant insubordination . . . I mean, you come in here reeking of booze 3 out of 5 days . . . its fucking enough!' He hit the desk again, this time with a closed fist. 'It's been over 2 years since your brother died for Christsakes. You need to move on now!' Kevin leaned back in his chair and puffed his cheeks out. He let out a long, slow breath. Right away, right after he said it, he wished he hadn't, not like that anyway, but his emotions got the best of him.

Danny sat silently; his stare began to pierce through Kevin's chest. His jaw hardened as he clenched his teeth so hard that he thought they might crack. Danny felt the blood rush to his head and the dizziness that comes with adrenaline releasing suddenly and intensely. He fought hard against it in order to swallow his rage back down. He began to see red and flickering stars. His mouth had been stripped of any saliva. Finally, after a few aching seconds, he felt his lungs give way and he took in a deep breath. When he let it out, he felt the fury begin to dissipate. He raised his eyes finally to meet Kevin's. Kevin's own face showed signs of a struggle to remain firm. Danny could tell it was also masking some fear and he thought perhaps some sorrow as well.

Danny stood up abruptly from the chair and picked up the letter from the desk. He folded it and put it back into the envelope. He turned and began to walk out, but took two steps towards the door and turned back to the face Kevin again. He said quietly, 'Killed'.

Kevin looked up at Danny and asked 'What's that

Dan?'

'My brother didn't die Kevin. . . He was killed.'

Kevin's face hardened and his eyes glanced down to the floor, then back to Danny's. He shook his head slowly in acknowledgment, 'Ya, I know Dan . . . I know'.

Danny raised the letter to his forehead in a mock salute and left Kevin's office then. He walked into his own office and grabbed his coat off the hook. He walked out and stepped into the open elevator and stuffed the letter into his pocket. He took the elevator down to the ground floor and walked back through reception towards the exit. The same receptionist gave him another funny look. Danny held up his middle finger at her as he walked past and said, 'mind your fucking business' before leaving brusquely through the rotating doors.

Danny crossed the tram tracks on Harcourt Street to head for the bar across the street. He paused when he reached the stairs and thought better of going in, 'too likely I'd run into someone from work' he thought. He decided to walk for a little while to see if he could calm himself down. He started up Harcourt Street towards Stephen's Green. He tried to lose himself in the walk by focusing on the lines of brick buildings on both sides of the street. He remembered how quaint he thought they were when he first moved over. Much of Dublin, at least the parts that looked like this, reminded him of Beacon Hill in Boston. 'All built by the Brits most likely' he thought 'It's too bad much of the old offices that inhabited these areas fell victim to the fizzled out economy'. It didn't exactly fizzle out in Ireland actually it was more like it reached the peak then started free falling . . . the celtic tiger declawed' he mused to himself.

When he reached the first gate in Stephen's Green, he entered the park and slowed his pace. Despite the Irish weather, there were plenty of people wandering within, most likely out of the office to stretch the legs and grab coffee to hold them over until lunch.

Danny walked on through the center of the park past the fountain and found an empty seat on the bench that looked across a landscaped green. He dug into his inside pocket and pulled out his phone, 'No missed calls, no messages . . . Christ, not even an email.' He wondered if he had already successfully alienated everyone he knew. Michelle wouldn't talk to him, his mother only depressed him more, his father . . . well, no chance there. Maybe Jim was his only link back to his old life . . . his real life. 'Maybe after all, my brother was the only one that cared' he thought. He wished silently that he would have been a better brother, but it was too late now. There was no chance at redemption as far as he could see. Revenge still stirred in his stomach however. As soon as he thought this, he was interrupted by a sudden clang on the other side of the bench. He looked over to his right and saw that it was a plastic bag with a couple of loose tall beer cans that made the noise. The man carrying it could barely hold himself up long enough to turn around and plop his backside on the bench. Danny crinkled his nose at the immediate waft of odor that floated his way. It was a mix of slime and stale booze that only a homeless heroin addict could perfect. Danny looked at the man. He had a hood up over a wind-blown red face and dirty reddish hair and eyebrows. He might've weighed a max 120lbs with all his clothes on. Danny thought, 'he's a long way from the Quays on the Liffey, must be a wanderer.'

Danny took his new neighbor's presence as a cue to leave and gathered himself before standing up. The man grunted something that Danny couldn't make out, nor had he cared to. He just kept walking, this time out of the park and down to Grafton Street. He turned right after a block or two down Grafton

Street and headed straight to a pub called Keogh's that had grown quite familiar to him over the last year. When he sat at the bar and ordered a Guinness, it dawned on him that really his stroll in the park was nothing more than a distraction. It was just something to do until the clock struck noon, nothing more, nothing less. For a second this thought left him with a guilty feeling. Within seconds . . . it had drifted.

22 MIKE RIORDAN

'Daddy! Daddy!' Rebecca yelled to her father while kicking the heels of her feet against her plastic car seat in the back of Mike's Quad cab pickup truck. 'Are we going to the plaza?' she asked in her junior Boston accent.

'You know what she's gonna ask' Mike's wife Elaine said while smiling and rolling her eyes. 'You'll notice she never dares to ask me. She's too used to me saying no.'

Mike finished leveling out the truck in his parking spot and put the transmission into Park. He winked at Elaine as he turned around to face his daughters Rebecca and Ashley. 'Yes, we're here at the plaza Becky, just like we said, so Mommy can go shopping.'

'She wants ice cream Dad!' Mike's older daughter Ashley said with a look that said she couldn't be bothered with such childish requests. 'She always does!'

'Not always!' Becky shouted, 'just Brigham's'.

Elaine turned around then and gave the girls a look that said 'No Anything if the yelling keeps up'. It was a look they both knew well.

'Okay, Okay girls, maybe if you stick by us the whole time while Mom does her shopping, you'll be rewarded with some Brighams' Mike said as he climbed out of the Driver's seat and opened the back door to get Becky out of her chair.

'Thanks Daddy, we won't run away' Becky assured him as he helped her out of the chair. He took her hand then in his and locked the doors as they walked towards the entrance.

They walked into the plaza through the main entrance at the front of the parking lot. Mike was glad to see the mall wasn't too busy, at least not busy for a Thursday, which could generally be hectic. Living close by and living with just his wife and his girls, a one-man show, meant Mike spent more time at the plaza than he cared to admit.

Elaine had insisted that he came along this time.

Since he'd been picking up side work to balance off the Union layoffs, they hadn't had much time to do things as a family. It wasn't an ideal day out for either of them, but they had a wedding to go to for a cousin of Elaine's the following week. Therefore she needed a new dress to wear. 'P.O.L.R.' Mike thought, 'Path of Least Resistance. Plus, it wasn't so bad, there was plenty of kids play areas in the mall these days.' At least the girls could run around and enjoy themselves, even if shopping made him miserable.

Elaine led them through a few shops, then decided after an hour of disappointments that she'd be much faster on her own. She went off to the Nordstrom woman's section, while Mike agreed to head to down to Brigham's and feed the girls while they waited for her to pick out a dress.

Mike made his way towards the escalator with his two girls in tow. He stood in front of the escalator and made each child get a grip of the railing. At the bottom of the ramp they made a 180 degree turn towards Brigham's Ice cream parlor. When Becky saw the sign, she started to pick up her pace and Mike felt his hand jerk forward slightly as she tried to run. 'Relax baby, we'll get there soon enough' Mike said to her. They passed a shoe store and Mike peered into the window as he continued to walk trying to see the price tag on a pair of Chippewa boots in the front window.

He stopped quickly as two teenage girls nearly knocked him over, walking passed quickly, both staring at their respective cell phones.

Mike found himself staring in front of a book store entrance as he recovered his footing. 'A book signing must be on' he thought, 'awfully busy for a store with just books in it.' As he looked into the store at the group of people lining up, he couldn't help feeling a sense of familiarity. The guy signing the books, presumably the writer looked really familiar to Mike, but he couldn't place him.

Mike stood still for a minute, and finally it struck him who he was looking at. He noticed the billboard in the window, 'Meet Boston's own Brendan Maguire.'

It was a name that Mike knew intimately. That name had crossed his mind through day dreams and nightmares alike. Mike froze when it all came together for him. He didn't know what to do. Finally, he had to succumb to his daughters' impatience as they both frantically pleaded with him to keep walking. He moved slowly, more deliberately towards Brigham's and walked in and slid into a booth and just stared blankly.

Elaine paid for her new dress by credit card in Nordstrom's. At the register they asked for her zip code, she always felt violated when they did that. Market research is way too in your face nowadays.

She lugged her bags onto the escalator and breathed a deep sigh of relief that her shopping was done. She found a nice dress that fit well, without breaking the bank. This was nearly a cause for celebration.

When she walked into the restaurant the hostess with the funny pointed hat directed her to the booth where her family was sitting. She walked through the seating area and found the girls with Mike sitting in the second-to-last booth. There were chicken finger plates with French fries in front of each of her daughters, which seemed normal. She saw nothing in front of Mike which seemed strange. Also, his complexion was pale and there was a distant look across his face. Elaine slid herself next to Ashley on the booth and across from Mike. 'Are you feeling okay hon, you aren't looking too well?' She asked.

'Huh?' Mike said, looking up at her as if he just realized she was there. 'Oh, yeah. Sorry, was just thinking about something.'

'You're not eating? That's not like you.'

'Not hungry babe, I'll get something later maybe.' Mike raised his hand and got the waiter's attention to give a signal for the bill.

'We're leaving? I haven't eaten yet.' Elaine said confused.

'Sorry' Mike said, 'I forgot, I gotta call from Domenic, the guy I was doing some work with. I have to go price a roofing job.'

'First I heard of it, I thought this was a family day today?' Elaine asked, openly showing her irritation.

'I know honey, I'm sorry, like I said, I forgot about it. I'll leave you money to order something.'

'It's not about the money, forget it Mike . . . whatever.'

Mike paid the bill and got a quart of ice cream and some hot fudge to go so his daughters were kept happy. He still wasn't quite sure what he was going to do, but he knew he had to get his family home and had to be alone to think for a minute.

It only took about 10 minutes to get to their house, including the time it took to carry Becky into the house and put her on the couch for her nap. He tried to appear normal but it was difficult to do this with so many thoughts racing through his head. After getting the girls inside he grabbed his work folder and tape measure to keep up the charade and hustled to get out of the house.

23 MIKE AND BRENDAN

Mike drove directly back to the plaza and parked right outside the front entrance. The parking lot had already started to clear out as the families out shopping for the day loaded up their cars and left. He sat in his truck for what seemed like an hour, but was probably more like 10 minutes, just trying to figure out what to do.

Mike decided to pull into a parking space and walk back inside. He entered the plaza again through the front doors still unsure what he was planning. He just knew that he should at least get one more look at the kid to be sure it was him.

When he got back to the book store however, he found the grates lowered and the shop all but empty.

It had closed in his absence. He felt a rush of anger for a brief moment, but it flamed out quickly and gave way to a strange feeling of relief. 'Maybe it was better this way' he thought.

He realized he was loitering and probably drawing attention to himself, so he headed back towards the way he came in. As he walked towards the exit, he glanced into the Bar & Grill that was attached to the mall. It was definitely still open, there were a good few people in having an early dinner. He stopped walking when once again he had a feeling of familiarity sweep over him. He put his face all the way up against the glass this time to be sure. He stared right into the eyes of Brendan Maguire, sitting alone at a tall table with a coffee in front of him. Brendan saw Mike, but made no movement to leave. In fact he kept eye contact as best he could. Mike was hit with lightheadedness momentarily, but he blinked it away as he entered the restaurant. He walked past the smiling hostess and ignored her greeting. He crossed the bar area and only stopped when he reached Brendan's table.

Brendan was in a tall chair, so even with Mike standing, they were still roughly eye level. They remained in their places for about 15 seconds before Mike finally let out a deep breath. His shoulders drooped noticeably as he did so, his posture going from hunter to victim in one motion. Brendan held out his palm towards a chair in a gesture for Mike to sit down. Mike glanced sideways back at him, but still pulled the chair over and took a seat.

'Do you want a drink or anything?' Brendan asked.

Mike said nothing but shook his head 'No'.

'What's that you're drinking?' Mike asked.

'Just coffee' Brendan answered. 'I don't drink much really.'

Mike nodded like he was agreeing with something Brendan said. 'I often thought about what I'd do if I ever ran into you.'

Brendan just kept looking at Mike, letting him go on in his own time. 'I always told myself I'd kill you ya know . . . Never thought about how or when . . . just thought that I'd do it. Even bought a gun . . . sits there in my closet just haunting me.'

Brendan's expression didn't change, but he paused for about 30 seconds, 'can't say I'd blame you if you did.'

'Yeah, well. I'm not gonna kill you . . . I think we both know that.'

Brendan nodded his head slightly reassured.

'Why did it take until now to run into you? I heard

you got out a while ago?' Mike asked.

'I couldn't take moving back here.' Brendan answered and reached for his coffee. He took a sip and continued. 'My publisher had to beg me to make an appearance. This is actually the first time back home since I was out.'

'I see . . . staying long?' Mike asked.

Brendan shook his head 'No', 'I fly out before the weekend's over.'

Mike raised his eyebrows, 'short trip then I guess. Where you flying too? Or are you keeping it close to your chest?'

'No, it's no secret. I'm not hiding Mike, I've accepted that I may reap what I sow at some point. I'm living just outside Philly.'

'Many writers out that way?' Mike asked.

'Writers? . . . Not that I know. I wrote once, that's all. Might write again, but I'm not rushing into it. I work out there though . . . well volunteering any way.'

Mike nodded, 'Soup kitchen or something?'

'Nah. No soup kitchen. I work with teenagers just out of Juvy. Started off as part of my parole, but I've kept it on since. It's not much, but I guess it makes me feel like I'm giving back something. Probably not what you want to hear I know.'

Mike lightened his mood suddenly. 'Hmm, sounds like a tough gig man. Dealing with groups of thugged-out teenagers, I'm sure it ain't easy.'

Brendan shook his head slightly. 'Wasn't easy at first definitely, but it's gotten easier. I've gotten better at it. It's funny actually, it was something Jim taught me that got me through the first while. I asked Jim once how he kept his staff in line without being a totalitarian . . . a good few hard-necks put in time at the deli. He told me about an experience he had back when he was 17 or 18 working with kids in the Quincy rec gyms . . . Sterling middle school I think. He said he showed up the first day and got pushed, spat at and everything else by a few of the wise-ass kids in the gym. He was almost afraid at first, he wasn't much older than those kids ya know . . . and he was extremely outnumbered. He didn't know what to do with them. He went home after the evening rec time and thought about how to approach the next time he dealt with them. He thought about the group and began to think about a few of the kids that stood out . . . there were maybe two or three who . . . didn't look like the ring leaders or anything, but when they spoke the others listened. He remembered that the other guys, those trying to cause trouble, would do something wise and then look to them for some kind of approval. So Jim said he made it his goal the next few gym sessions to try and get to know these few . . . talk to them, see what made them tick. He said he just knew if he could get those few guys on side he might have a chance with the rest. So that's what he did. He won over those two-three kids. He got them on his side, and immediately he noticed the change in the group. By the end, that group of young kids grew to love Jim . . . grew to respect him . . . and he always talked about that being one of his favorite experiences. So . . . I basically tried the same approach. It works . . . not always, but mostly, it works. I guess that's kind of like my homage to Jim. . . Sorry Mike . . . I carry on a bit . . . and I . . . I know you don't need to hear this.'

Mike pushed back in his seat and winced as he made to get up . . . painful joints. His eyes were glistening. At some point while Brendan spoke, tears formed in Mike's eyes that he fought back. 'Actually Brendan . . . I think maybe I needed to hear something like that.' He rubbed his eyes with his fingers, 'My family's waiting for me. I should get home.' Mike tucked in his chair and started to walk away.

Brendan called out lightly, 'hey Mike.'

Mike turned and looked at him again.

'I am sorry.'

Mike pursed his lips for a second and swallowed. 'I know you are kid.' Mike left the bar then and walked back to his truck. As he started it up, he smiled at the thought of his family and just as suddenly felt a wave of loss as his cousin Jim crossed his mind again.

24 BRENDAN

Brendan's hands shook as he watched Mike leave the restaurant and walk over to his truck, his large builders' frame eclipsing most of the view from the inside out of the window. He surely dodged a bullet on that one. Brendan thought, 'it wouldn't take much effort for a man of that size and strength to inflict pain'. He reddened with shame as he thought about their encounter while Mike's truck circled the parking lot to find the exit. Although he felt a weight lift from his shoulders as the light turned green and he watched the truck head left towards Braintree's five corners and disappear from his sight. His instructions were pretty clear and they included nothing about trying to bury the hatchet with Jim Carson's best friend. When he noticed Mike through the bookstore window however, standing there entranced, solid as a statue with his daughters in tow, he felt like now was his one and only chance to give the man the opportunity to seek any closure necessary.

He withheld the urge to breathe a strong sigh of relief once he realized Mike was someone without a lust for pure revenge, at least not without weighing the consequences. Brendan siphoned much of his dwindling courage to keep a cool head and wait out Mike's approach, which he knew would happen.

As Brendan signaled for the bill from the waiter, his stress levels began to rise again with the thought of the next couple of days. 'This is only level one in this game of which I'm just a pawn' he thought. He checked the time on his watch and tried to figure how much time he would have to get back to his hotel. His instructions were to do his one appearance, and then haul ass back to the hotel and stay put until his services were needed. No cellphones were the rule apparently, so he was going to be forced to stay locked in the room under a bogus name waiting for a phone call that may or may not come in the next few days. 'Oh, also don't forget the kicker . . . what will actually be needed when and if that call does come is still to be communicated. Consider it a mystery.' Brendan thought to himself as he laid down enough cash to cover his bill plus tip, 'Same slave . . . different master.'

25 DANNY ON EDGE

Danny didn't leave the pub for the rest of the day. Even when the daytime crowd left and the after work patrons gathered in he didn't wrap it up. He wasn't drinking quickly, but he was drinking steadily. After a few hours of pouring pints of Guinness down his throat, the cotton-mouth finally got to him. He ordered a pint glass of water and took it down in two gulps. The coldness gave him a frozen headache and he winced with pain.

When he started to feel tired and dizzy, he switched from pints to captain and cokes. The captain was sweeter and easier to swallow and the coke gave him the caffeine boost to keep him upright. He had been there for hours. Luckily for him the bartenders had changed shifts a couple times, so it wasn't as obvious to them that he hadn't moved from his seat.

Pretty soon, the lights were dimmed and the music came on in the background, which caused the chatter volume to increase as well. The caffeine's kick only lasted momentarily, so Danny eventually grew tired again. Throughout the afternoon he had been checking his phone constantly, holding out hope that Michelle would call or text. As the afternoon faded into evening his patience with waiting dimmed at the same rate. He dialed Michelle's number a few times, but it went straight to voicemail. He followed the calls up with texts, but there was never any response. As his head began to increase in weight and nod forward, he decided he'd had enough. He stuffed his phone back into his pocket and closed out his tab.

He slid his chair back and stood up and felt a sudden onslaught of dizziness. He stumbled forward and fell into a group of guys standing in a semi-circle around a ledge against the wall. 'Sorry' Danny slurred as he tried to right himself. One of the guys, a stocky man with strawberry blond hair and a scarf around his neck took exception to Danny bumping into him and spilling his drink.

He turned and shoved Danny making him sway

backwards and fall into another table. Danny climbed back up apologizing to the table of girls he landed on. When he was on his feet again, he walked by the group of guys again, who were now looking at him in amusement.

'Fucking take it easy asshole, it was an accident.' Danny said to the guy with the scarf.

'Oh! He's a focking yank!' the guy in the scarf shouted in his South Dublin accent, looking to his friends for approval.

Danny stood still for a second. Feeling slowly crawled back to his limbs as the adrenaline seemed to counteract his drunkenness. He smiled at the table and pretended to join in the laughter. 'Yank huh? That's funny.' Danny made like he was going to walk past, but then spun his left foot in a pivot and threw a left hook that hit the scarf guy square in the mouth. The punch knocked the guy into his friends crying and bleeding all over his scarf. One of the other friends threw a punch at Danny, but he pulled his left arm back to cover his face immediately like a boxer. The blow hit him in the bicep and he countered with a quick right cross to the man's face that drew blood from the nose.

The fight caused the people in the pub to scatter,

leaving an opening for two bouncers to grab Danny by the arms from behind. Other guys from the table tried to get in to punch Danny but he fended them off with kicks to the groin and face before they could get in close.

The bouncers dragged Danny out front, going hard through the double doors, almost knocking over a couple of patrons on their way into the bar. A third bouncer, presumably the doorman, ran out to Dawson Street and flagged down a taxi, which is where the two others deposited Danny. Danny ceased his tirade once they got him outside. He went quietly into the back of the taxi and just told the driver, 'Harold's Cross.'

'Okay' said the driver, 'early night?' she asked smirking at the sight of Danny from the rearview mirror. Danny, had been looking at himself in the rearview, eyeballing the small cut on the corner of his mouth that was bleeding slightly. His gaze drifted across to the eyes of the driver in the rear view when she spoke. 'Woah' Danny said.

'What do you mean woah?' She answered quickly.

'Sorry, I didn't know they had female taxi drivers. That's all, you caught me by surprise.'

'That's right mister, we can vote now and

everything' She said sarcastically in a fake American accent.

'I meant no disrespect miss, sorry. Actually, it's a compliment. You're the prettiest taxi driver I've ever seen.' He said and smiled into the rearview mirror.

The driver met his eyes in the mirror and arched an eyebrow. 'Is that the same charm that got you that bloody lip?'

'Hey, love hurts. Haven't you heard that before?'

'Yes I have and I've lived it.' She answered.

'Can I ask you a question?' Danny asked

'You just did.' She replied.

'Funny . . . hey, does your boyfriend mind you driving a taxi on the night shift?'

'I don't have a boyfriend. Plus I'm not on the night shift. It's still early and you're my last fare. Pretty loaded question from a guy with a wedding ring on his finger. You're married I'm guessing.'

'Was . . . well . . . am married, but separated. She doesn't speak to me anymore.'

'Really? You look too young to be separated.'

'That's what I told her! Didn't work though, she still left me anyway.'

'Could've been the bar fights.' She said and winked at him in the mirror. 'You seem to be taking it well though.'

'I'm drunk . . . it helps. And it was more likely the drinking, neglect and womanizing that did me in.'

The taxi driver laughed out loud and had to ease onto the brakes. 'Jesus, you're awfully direct. Not an ounce of shame on you.'

'I'm American . . . I don't know any better.' Danny answered. 'So honestly, why do you drive a cab? A young girl in Dublin, surely there's plenty more jobs out there.'

'If you must know, I have a young son to take care of and I needed a job. So, here's my job for the moment.'

'I knew you had someone. Too pretty to be alone' He said.

'You're relentless' She said.

'And handsome.' He answered. As they took a left off the Grand Canal onto Harold's Cross road, he pointed to his apartment. 'There's my place, with the light on.'

She pulled into the small drive and pointed to the meter. Danny handed her a 20 and said to keep the change. He leaned closer to the front and she finally turned towards him. Danny read it as a signal of interest. 'Let me make you a drink.' Danny said.

'What!' she said in surprise. 'I'm working and that work is driving a taxi. How can I drink?'

'You just told me I was your last fare. So how 'bout it?' He answered.

She looked at him with squinted eyes, a funny look, but Danny thought, not without interest.

'You're a stranger. I don't even know your name. Where's the funny accent from anyway?'

'I'm Danny Carson. I grew up in Boston. Now I live right there.' He pointed again to the apartment. 'Come on, one drink . . . maybe two. If you get too drunk, don't worry I'll call you a cab. I know a really good driver.' He said while plastering a large toothy smile on his face.

She smiled. 'Okay Danny Carson. A drink it is then.'

She didn't even give him the chance to take his keys out of the lock before she kissed him. By the time they reached the bedroom, Danny had already tripped twice over a shoe and had the first four buttons from his favorite shirt torn off the front.

. . . .

The next morning came quickly for Danny. When he woke up, his mouth was sealed shut with dryness and his head had a freight train running through it. He was alone again, with no sign of the mysterious taxi girl. 'She never did get that drink' He thought, 'Must've had somewhere to be.' He got up to go the bathroom. While washing his hands, he noticed how swollen his left hand had gotten. Flashes of the altercation the night before ran through his head. He found an ice pack in his freezer and popped it over his hand and tied it down with a dish towel. He didn't bother looking at his phone. He knew there'd be no messages from Michelle.

He poured a glass of club orange and took it over to his table. 'It's time' he thought to himself 'I've waited long enough.' He opened up his laptop and turned the machine on. When it started up, he cringed at the wallpaper on the screen's background. It was a picture of him and Michelle on Rosnowlagh beach in Donegal. 'Feels like a different life' he thought.

He opened up the internet explorer and typed in the web address for Aer Lingus's website. He booked a ticket to leave for Boston the next day.

Once it was booked, he went and found his pants on the floor next to his bed. He found his phone in the pocket and typed in, 'I fly in tomorrow. 3pm. Danny' and sent the text to Mike and his mother.

....

Mike heard the text in the early hours of the morning, but didn't check it until he was up. When he read it, he said silently 'I guess it's going to happen'. The call Mike made next was brief. When the man answered, Mike simply said, Danny flies in tomorrow. My guess is that you have 48 - 72 hours before he does something he regrets.'

The man responded, 'As expected then. Appreciate the heads up Mike.'

'Yeah, well, you know who I'm doing it for.' Mike answered, and then hit end call on his phone. Next he erased the number from his call history.

26 FLYNN MCBRIDE

Flynn stopped on the makeshift wooden steps to readjust his grip and wipe the sweat from his forehead with the back of his forearm. He couldn't remember being in such bad shape. The back and forth carrying of tools up to the landing had his leg muscles aching and his lungs nearly wheezing.

He put the nail gun set down from his right hand so he could readjust the table under his left arm. If the foreman saw him, he'd definitely get an earful for carrying too much up at once. Then again, if the carpenter's steward saw him, his foreman would probably hear it from him since the laborers were supposed to have everything setup before the carpenters even clocked in.

Not that it mattered, but it wasn't his fault that there was an accident that morning heading into the city. With that, plus the random road works, traffic was worse than normal.

Once he got his grip back and his breath, he bent down and reached for the nail gun to start up the steps again. He could hear some noise coming from up top and heard one of the carpenters yelling for his gear, 'Probably that loud mouth Lentini' Flynn thought, 'he never shuts his fucking trap.'

'Two seconds!' Flynn shouted back and double timed it up the last few steps to the landing. When he got to the top, he saw Lentini standing back looking impatient. His belt was on, but his hard hat was turned backwards and he was lighting a cigarette, which indicated he was taking a break. A much younger man, who looked to be an apprentice stood next to Lentini and looked like he was trying to do his best imitation.

'Bout fucking time you showed up McBride, its nearly fucking coffee.' Lentini cackled to himself and his sidekick did the same, exaggerating the joke's actual effect to please his mentor.

Flynn placed the nail gun case down and struggled with the table saw for a moment. 'You don't look too fucking pushed Lentini . . . I thought you couldn't smoke on the premises?'

Lentini shrugged his shoulders with indifference, 'Who's fucking smoking?' He looked to his apprentice, 'you smell smoke kid?'

Laughing too loudly again, the kid shook his head no. 'See McBride, no one's smoking, what are you gonna rat me out? That'd get you shanked in prison . . . but I guess I don't gotta tell YOU that.' Lentini stressed.

'Fuck you' Flynn answered and looked around for somewhere to put down the table saw. He looked over at Lentini, 'Where's the best place to put this?' he said holding up the saw.

'Usually on the table setup on the saw horses, but my fucking laborer never set them up this morning.'

Flynn sighed heavily 'Right' he said and placed the saw on the ground next to the nail gun. 'I'll be right up with them.' Flynn turned to head back down the stairs again. 'Take your fucking time McBride. We're paid by the hour here anyway.' The apprentice laughed out loud this time. At least this time his amusement was genuine.

Flynn headed down the stairs, faster this time and fumed more and more with each step down. The laughter seemed to decrease in volume and he eventually put it out of his mind.

Flynn got pretty much straight into demo work after that. On another section of the job site he and a few other laborers were called over and handed sledge hammers, crowbars and little white dust masks. They were tasked with clearing out and taking down an old decrepit bungalow, or at least that's what it was as far as they could tell. One of the guys said it was most likely an old rectory for a parish that no longer existed. Holy or not, it wasn't owned by the Church anymore and either way, it was coming down.

Most of the laborers were not happy with demo duty, especially when it involved old dusty buildings, but Flynn relished the opportunity to release some of his aggression. He went straight for it, swinging his hammer at full tilt and digging the dagger end through some old wood paneling, nearly tearing the wall off in one fevered tug. Next, he bust through as much wood framing as he could with the hammer, then pried off the remainder with a heavy crowbar.

Others took short breaks, either to smoke or chat. Flynn kept at it however and many of the guys showed flashes of intimidation at his violent spectacle. Flynn had moved on to the sledge hammer to take out the concrete base when he finally stopped for a breath. At that time he noticed that many of the others had dropped their tools and those with belts dropped them in place. Flynn realized it was time for lunch. He reluctantly leaned the sledge hammer against what remained of the wall. He reached to his face and pulled the mask down from his mouth and let it hang around his neck. The lingering dust started to creep into his lungs immediately, so he cupped his hand over his nose and mouth and headed toward the opening to follow the others out.

When he reached the outside, everyone had already dispersed. He hadn't expected that anyone would wait for him or anything, the Union could be as bad as high school as far as cliques were concerned. Flynn had eaten alone almost every day since he started the job, 'why should today be any different?' He thought. He headed off the site to cross Huntington Ave over to the small parking area outside a bar called the Squealing Pig. He unlocked his truck and reached behind his seat for the mini cooler that held his lunch. He walked around back and dropped the tailgate to his beaten down pickup truck.

He propped himself up on the bench and took a deep breath once he had settled. As he opened the cooler and began tucking into his lunch, he heard the chatter of voices and saw a group of carpenters and a few laborers sneaking into the Squealing Pig. 'Another liquid lunch' he thought 'at least I don't need to rush back. God knows those fuckers won't.' Flynn couldn't help from seething with jealousy when he thought of that group of guys drinking some beers over lunch. He hadn't had so much as a drink since he was released. His sobriety was a parole requirement and he was in West Quincy twice a week pissing into a cup for drug testing. He'd been clean for a couple months at least, but the lure to stray was constant. This only added to his aggression, which was fierce to begin with.

Flynn hated bending to anyone's rules, but his old man had called in several favors to get him sprung as soon as he did. He also set him up with the Union for his job. Out of work cocaine dealers were not exactly marketable . . . not in any field.

Flynn took about twenty minutes for lunch. He lit a smoke while packing up the truck and walked slowly back to the site to give himself enough time to enjoy it. When he got back to work there were noticeably fewer people around and those that had stuck it had tailed off and worked at a slower pace. 'Start nothing new after 2' he had often heard some of the guys say with a touch of pride. Flynn didn't find those quips funny, but he couldn't argue with the motto. When it came down to it, he hated working. He only hustled through his work because it made the time go by faster so he could leave.

After a slow couple of hours, the clock hit 3:30 and the laborers stopped for the day. Flynn had started wrapping up his tools for the day when he heard a commotion outside. He peaked out to see a couple of men yelling at each other and being held back by a few guys from attacking the one another. Apparently one of the carpenters thought he'd speed the day along by lifting and stacking some of the 2x4's to store for the night. The labor steward took exception and laid into him . . . something about letting the laborers stick to the labor and carpenters stick to hammering shit. 'Fucking politics' Flynn thought, 'just like fucking prison' everyone at each other's throats; carpenters and laborers arguing with each other, stopping only to make fun of the plumbers and electricians, who were apparently 'primadonnas' mainly because they wanted a clean workspace. 'Fuck it' Flynn thought, 'Let 'em beat each other's' heads in, free entertainment anyway.'

Flynn walked around the mayhem and dropped his demo-tools off over at the cages. He flicked off his hard hat once he left the gates of the job site and headed across the avenue back to his truck. He found the keys dug into one of his deep Carhatt pockets and opened up the truck. He lifted the seat back and popped his hard hat and work jacket in the fold behind the driver's seat. He lit a cigarette just as he sat in and shut the door. He struggled to roll the manual window down quickly as the smoke began to sting his eyes. He took a heavy drag from the butt when the window was open and sighed loudly as he exhaled. Getting home in the evening was almost always the toughest part of his day. Traffic going south on 93 was brutal every day. It was the only time he ever considered making friends at work, to carpool and use the H.O.V. lane. He'd have chanced it anyway alone if he wasn't already on thin ice with law enforcement. 'The Staties were always setup to catch the chancers anyway.' He thought.

He found a classic rock station that was more music than talk and headed off on his journey. As expected the highway traffic was crawling from South Station to Dorchester. It didn't open up until a little while after the JFK exit.

He jumped off the highway two exits later onto Adams Street. During his hour in the truck he had talked to Dora and told her he'd come by her place with a pizza for dinner. By the time he picked the pizza up in Lower Mills, it was nearly cold. He paid for it and headed around the corner to Dora's apartment. He decided to leave the truck in the spot he took in the CVS parking lot and walk to Dora's since on street parking was tough to find in front of her place.

He glanced over at his truck as he tried to remember if he'd locked it. He was hit with a feeling of déjà vu when he saw an 80's model Buick parked next to his truck. It was familiar for some reason, but he couldn't place it.

He decided it stood out simply because of its newness. For a 25 year old car, it looked like it was just driven from the manufacturer. That was odd to him. 'Fuck it' he thought, 'pizza's already cold, better get to Dora's'. Then he took off down the street.

27 DORA'S PLACE

Flynn walked up the front steps to Dora's place. He balanced the pizza on top of his left hand and reached to open the screen door with his right. He flung the door open and shoved his hip against it to keep it from springing back. The main door was ajar so he leaned his elbow against it to prop it open more. 'Dora!' he yelled, 'you home? I'm coming in.'

Flynn walked into the apartment which opened into a spacious living room. Dora peaked her head out of the bedroom door, with a cordless phone held to her ear. She gave Flynn the 'one minute' signal and pointed to the kitchen.

Flynn walked through the living room and over to the kitchen. It was more like a kitchenette since it was open and pretty much the same room as the living room except for the open doorway. He placed the pizza box on the table and opened it up to take a slice. He found some paper plates on the counter and took out a couple slices and dropped them onto a plate for Dora. He took his first bite while standing over the sink when Dora came back into the room. The pizza was kind of cold, but still tasted excellent.

'Standing over the sink doesn't mean you don't need a plate. I'll have mice if you keep that up.' Dora said to Flynn.

Flynn replied with pizza still being chewed in his mouth, 'hate to break it to you, but you probably already do. All these old houses have 'em.'

'Yeah but you don't need to leave a trail of crumbs directly to my kitchen for them. Give them a challenge at least.' Dora said as she took her plate and a Pepsi from the refrigerator. She jumped up then onto a stool at the kitchen counter. 'Ugh' she said when she looked at the pizza, plain cheese . . . you mean to tell me of all the toppings around, you just stuck with plain cheese? How adventurous of you.'

Flynn shrugged, 'I'm a minimalist when it comes to pizza . . . Base, sauce and cheese. That's all.'

Dora sighed loudly, 'Yeah, I've heard your 'less is

more' talk in relation to pizza a million fucking times at this point, I got it. Still, you could've gotten half and half.'

'Maybe next time' Flynn added.

Dora took a bite from her slice, 'Ahh, its fucking cold too! You're on fire today.'

'Traffic sucked, you know how it gets in the afternoons. Hey, what's up with you swearing so much? Makes you sound . . . I don't know . . . trashy or something. You should quit that.'

'Well if it isn't the pot calling the kettle black . . . anyway, when you're brother's a jail bird, it comes with the territory. I could talk like Jackie Kennedy and people'd still call me trash.'

'Hey, fucking watch it alright. I don't need to hear that shit from you.'

'Language Flynn? Hypocrisy doesn't suit you.'

'Fine forget I said shit then.' Flynn stopped talking and turned to open the refrigerator door. He stood with the door open, leaning on it trying to make a decision.

'Is there a reason you're wasting my electricity?' Dora asked 'Can I help you with something?'

'Yeah . . . any rootbeer?' Flynn asked as he crouched down for a closer look.

'Strangely enough, yeah I think I do have some. Check the bottom drawer, there should be some cans there. They must be yours, who the hell else drinks that crap.'

Flynn found the cans and grabbed one. He stood back up and closed the door, 'not my brand, but it'll do the trick.' He cracked open the can and took a long sip followed by an 'Ahhhh'.

'Whatever, weirdo' Dora said and went back to her pizza.

Flynn put another two slices on his plate and took those, along with his root beer, into the living room. He found a spot on the couch and pulled the coffee table closer towards him. 'So, who was that you were talking to when I walked in?'

Dora looked suddenly uncomfortable 'No one, a friend is all'.

Flynn crinkled his forehead in a confused face. 'What? What's that supposed to mean? I don't give a shit about any boyfriends, who was it, I'm just making conversation.'

'No one, I said' Dora said again, firmer this time.

'Stop being so fucking shady, now I'm curious, it was obviously someone that I shouldn't know about, so fucking what.'

'It's none of your business Flynn, I don't wanna hear it from you that's all.'

'What! Quit being a bitch, I was just asking. Now you can bet your ass you're gonna tell me. Who could you possibly be talking to that could piss me off? Unless it was our bitch of a mother or something.'

Dora's face reddened at the mention of her mother. Flynn picked up on it immediately and gasped. 'Don't even fucking tell me you've been talking to her? Please don't say it.' Flynn got up suddenly from his seat and folded his hands at the top of his head.

Dora seemed to shrink into her seat as he walked towards the kitchen. 'That was fucking Ma wasn't it' He yelled at Dora, 'don't tell me she's fucking back around here.'

'It was her' Dora answered 'and stop talking about her like that!' She yelled 'She's my mother too. I have a right to talk to her.'

'Does Dad know you're in contact with her?' Flynn asked with a raised voice.

'No, Dad doesn't know anything. It's none of his business either who I talk to. She's back now and she's different. She apologized . . . '

'Bull Fucking Shit Dora and you know it' Flynn

cut her off. 'How much money did you give her so far huh?'

'I didn't give her any money!' Dora screamed. 'I told you it's not like the other times. It's different now . . . she's different now.' Dora pleaded as her voice cracked with the onslaught of tears.

Flynn just shook his head in disbelief, 'Ya know something kid . . . you're fucking delusional. That bitch'll keep coming around you until she spots her chance to rob you blind. Take my word for it.' Flynn turned then and started walking to the door. 'I can't deal with this bullshit right now, good fucking luck to ya, you'll see.'

As he walked out the door, he slammed the heavy door behind him firmly and let the screen door slam shut as well for good measure. His head was still shaking in disgust as he pounded his way up the street to his truck while Dora peered through the living room window after him, cursing him for even showing up in the first place.

28 DANNY'S HOME AGAIN

The airplane shifted direction slowly. As it turned, a gleam of sun shone through the open cabin window. Danny felt the heat from the glare and saw deep red as the light hit his closed eyelids. He broke from his siesta and turned his head away from the glare. He rubbed his eyes to wake himself up. He had drifted in and out of consciousness throughout the flight. Despite downing a number of over-the-counter sleeping tablets, he couldn't string together a consistent 6 hours of sleep. He woke several times from a multitude of nightmarish ramblings in his head that only slightly diminished in comparison to his real life anguish. Each time he woke up it was with a sudden jerk. The girl next to him no doubt wished the flight a hasty landing. She had relinquished the shared armrest without debate and had clung to the other neighbor's side. Whether or not they were travelling together didn't seem to factor into her decision.

Danny empathized with the girl, but it could've been worse, he thought, 'at least there's no stench of booze coming off me'. Although, he pondered whether the lack of booze in his system could have factored into his nightmares . . . brought on by the toxins leaving his bloodstream at last. He shut his eyes again, deciding to sleep again while he had the chance. As soon as he did, however, he felt a soft brush against his forearm. He opened his eyes again, this time to a woman in the turquoise green outfit of the airline staff. 'Excuse me sir' she said, 'we're now making our descent into Boston, could you please pull the seat back forward for landing and open the blind fully.'

Danny shook himself awake again, amused by the computer element to the woman's request. 'ah yes, thanks' he replied as he adjusted his seat forward. 'Excuse me, miss?' he asked the stewardess. 'Could you please tell me the local time?'

'Sure, it's 10 to 2 and we should be on the ground by 5 past.' She replied.

Danny nodded in thanks and took his watch from his wrist. He wound the hands back to set the watch to local time. He smiled slightly to himself and said quietly, 'it's like going back in time.' The young girl next to him hesitantly turned to him and asked 'Pardon? Did you ask me something?'

Danny looked at her slightly surprised at the interaction as he thought he'd said that only in his head. He answered, 'Sorry, was just saying to myself it's like going back in time . . . ya know . . . left at 2pm, land at 2pm, like the last few hours didn't happen.'

The girl scrunched her eyebrows and fought the urge to roll her eyes. Danny picked up on the disinterest and in an attempt to save face continued, 'Sorry, I must sound like a freak. I didn't realize I had said that out loud.' His face reddened slightly as he felt the blood rise to his cheeks in embarrassment. He just smiled apologetically and turned back to look out the window.

'Okay' she said and immediately dug into the inflight magazine. Danny sat back in his chair and now embarrassed, shared her wish for a fast landing. 'She must think I'm a psycho' he thought to himself. He popped a few pieces of chewing gum into his mouth and chewed feverishly. He swallowed his saliva every few seconds in hopes that his ears would pop and bring relief to his congested head, which felt ready to explode.

Once the plane touched down at Logan airport, Danny's thoughts about why he was here and what he was intending to do began to overwhelm him. He tried hard to push them away. He tried thinking of mundane things, like whether his bag would show up and how much a taxi would cost. The seriousness of his intentions could not be brushed aside however, and his conscience constantly nibbled away at his composure like a finicky child's approach to eating lunch. There were moments where he swore he could feel his soul disintegrating, pulled and dragged and melting away in the sun. He couldn't help but think of those Salvador Dalí paintings. 'Maybe that's what he meant when he stretched those clocks across the canvas' he thought to himself. He longed for the blind rage at times like these. 'At least rage would push me forward'.

As he approached the counter, the close-cropped man at passport control welcomed him home in what Danny felt was a sardonic demeanor. He shrugged off the non-insult and proceeded to baggage claim to collect his luggage. International baggage claim in

Logan airport never seemed to change. It was always the same lonely, sterile room, crawling with customs officers with 1990's hairstyles and sniffer dogs making the rounds. Danny allowed a chuckle to himself when he thought about the customs agents, had they all become a parody of themselves . . . transformed into walking cartoon characters.

He picked up his bag and walked over to the desk and handed the customs card to an officer. The man was no older than 30, but he had what looked like his father's moustache. The man looked Danny up and down for a moment, and then waved him through.

As he walked out to the arrivals hall, he saw throngs of friends and families eagerly awaiting the arrival of some loved one. Nostalgia gripped him as he remembered those times when Jim and his Mother had met him in that very hall. 'It had meant so little to me at the time' he thought 'funny how perspective changes you'. He headed through the crowd and found the exit to the taxi rank. The bite of the cold stung him as he walked outside. How easily he had forgotten the Boston winters. They are a different level of cold altogether. He greedily jumped into the first taxi available and rubbed his hands together to hurry up the warmth. 'Where to buddy?' the driver asked in that familiar twang that was like music to Danny's ears. 'Quincy Shore Drive' Danny answered, 'I don't know the exact address, but I know which house it is, so I can tell when we're near it.'

'Just yell "when" champ, I'll slow this jet down and you can barrel-roll outta here.' Danny laughed in response, happy to engage in some small talk to take his mind away from more damning thoughts. 'Thanks man' he answered, 'Glad I wore my hockey equipment now'.

29 KATHLEEN'S APARTMENT

Danny paid the taxi driver with a fifty dollar bill and told him to keep it. 'Big tip buddy, you sure?' the Driver replied honestly.

'Hey, you stopped the car long enough for me to walk out, it's the least I could do.' Danny replied.

The man nodded his approval and continued, well I'm much obliged then stranger, thanks a lot. May God watch over you.'

'Only when I'm sleeping, I hope.' Danny answered, 'Take it easy.' Then he jumped out and shut the door firmly behind him. The driver went to open the door to come around and get the bag from the trunk, but Danny waved him off, 'I got it man, watch your mirrors. Cars fly by on this street.' He pulled his bag out, a small dark duffel bag . . . just enough for a short trip. He flung it over his left shoulder and slammed the trunk to the old Ford shut with his right hand, tapping twice on the back to say goodbye like he was shooing a horse.

He crossed through the small parking lot, squeezing through a couple of tightly parked cars in the process, careful not to take a mirror or two with him. He paused at a set of twin doorways, hesitating to remember which apartment belonged to his mother. 'Has it been that long?' he asked himself.

He decided the porch with the wind-chimes could only belong to his mother, so he took the small steps to the door and rang the doorbell. He turned to look out at the street and thought 'cold and icy all day and the cars still whiz by both ways, one way speeding up to hit the bridge, the other way still lead-footed from the highway.'

He was making 'o's with his mouth and blowing out frost for about 30 seconds until he heard a lock switch open and chain being removed from the door. He peaked in to see a shadow through the door's glass-framed center. With one final sound of a bolt-lock being freed, the door opened slowly to reveal a familiar yet different face. It was a face that Danny knew so well, but one that also aged so much.

His mother's face had thinned greatly in such a short time. Danny thought, 'It had to have added 10 years to her appearance.' Also, her hair, once thick and auburn, was now shorter, still thick, but unmanaged and much grayer than he recalled. She smiled however, when she realized who had come to visit, and that smile at least had remained timeless, a permanent imprint on Danny's psyche.

'My son returns at last I see . . . and appears . . . what's the word? Stunned into submission and silence. Have I changed so greatly Danny that you've forgotten me? Or have you been struck dumb and mute by a greater power?' She asked slyly.

Danny smiled realizing at least that her wit had not failed her. 'Hi Mom, it's just that . . . your hair . . . um . . . your hair looks different. I don't remember it ever being so gray.'

'Well' she replied, 'it's been gray since you were 15 years old, I just lost interest in dying it. Maybe next time you visit, you'll give me more than a 24 hour notice and I'll have time to prepare myself to your standards. Now, get in the house before those ears catch frostbite, you were never a good listener at the best of times.' She said as she shoved open the door and turned to walk into the living room.

'Sorry Mom' Danny muttered. 'That was rude, you look great.'

She turned around to face him with flared nostrils and raised eyebrows. She put her arms around Danny and squeezed him tightly. 'Thanks Danny' she said, 'but lying won't get you far.'

Danny hugged her back and felt a feeling of guilt wash over him. He felt guilty for leaving . . . guilty for coming home. Pretty much, he felt guilty for everything.

After a time they both slowly backed away from their embrace. His mother turned around and headed through the hallway. Danny followed her into the apartment hall for a few steps until he branched off left into the living room, while she continued towards the kitchen. Danny slowed as he turned into the living room; his mother's voice sounding distant asked if he wanted something to eat. 'Yeah sure, anything thanks.' He answered.

Stepping into the room he noticed that although it was a different building, it was dressed up like a familiar family room he'd know through all his years growing up. The same charcoal gray, fabric couch with a hand knit afghan draped over the high back;

the same pine-wood stained rocking chair placed neatly under a tall reading lamp and angled to face the doorway and not the TV. Memories of Sunday mornings and snow days home from school swept over him as he entered the time capsule that was his Mother's living room.

He shut his eyes for a moment and could hear his mother clanging pots and dishes in the kitchen. 'She never could let anyone sleep once she was up.' He thought. He smiled to himself as he walked over to the fire place, catching a glimpse of himself in the mirror behind the mantelpiece.

The smile looked lost on his face or maybe it was more just unaccustomed to the motion, his facial muscles obviously out of practice.

In the mirror he looked much like he felt, tired and aged. His hairline hadn't yielded to time and the color hadn't gone gray, but his eyes looked worn. There were dark circles under his eyes and lines at the corner. Both looked of the permanent nature to him. Also, his formerly athletic neck and shoulders seemed to have softened under a layer of cushion that had gone surprisingly unnoticed until that point. His smile faded as he noticed the extent of the changes in himself and he averted his eyes from that dark stranger's reflection. His eyes moved to scan the framed photographs around the mantel, which for the most part chronicled his very existence. He focused in on a photo of he and Jim. It was one from Veteran's Stadium in Quincy from Jim's high school graduation. He remembered with painful clarity how he had rushed through the family's celebration afterwards. It was all so he could head off with some friends down to Cape Cod to celebrate finishing out the spring semester. 'Always so goddamn busy' he thought 'and for what? To suck down a 30-pack and watch fucking baseball with a bunch of guys I haven't seen or heard from in over 10 years.'

With his mind meandering through his conscience, he hadn't noticed that his Mother had stopped slamming dishes in the kitchen and stood behind him quietly in the doorway. She stood calmly watching him and finally she cleared her throat gently and spoke. 'Jim was glad you made it that day.' She said firmly trying to sound reassuring. 'It meant a lot to him.' Danny, slightly startled by her voice, noticed her behind him in the mirror only after she spoke. He looked away from the photo and turned to face her before sinking into the rocking chair and pushing off on his toes.

'Yeah, some brother I was. What did I stick around for . . . like 20 minutes?' He drew his hand up to his chin as a wrinkle of irritation ran across his brow.

His Mother stepped further into the room crouching down to meet his slouched posture at eye level while he slowed down his rhythm in the rocking chair. 'You were 20 years old Danny. That's what people do when they're 20 years old. They live in their own world. They have their own friends and their own lives. Don't think for a second that Jim didn't understand that, because he definitely did.'

'Oh, I'm sure he did.' Danny said with more venom than intended. 'Leave it to Jim to not hold a grudge for me being a lousy brother. Water off a duck's fucking back with him . . . always.'

His Mother left her crouched position and stood back up. She drew her hands to her hips and her face turned disapproving. 'You still don't get it do you Danny? You still don't understand. For a smart boy, you don't pick up an awful lot. You're always in a competition . . . Always!' She yelled. 'But, you're missing the point when it comes to Jim. He never held a grudge simply because you were his brother and he loved you . . . he got you. That's something you couldn't and I guess, still can't see for yourself.'

'Oh come off it Ma. What's there to get? What do I not get?' Danny asked.

'Mainly . . . my son . . . it's that you are and only ever were in competition with yourself. You . . . no one else. You're in some kind of race Danny and your moving fast. The only problem is, you don't realize that there's no one else around you. Not in front of you, not behind you. No one . . . nowhere. You're an island. I mean . . . just God help you sometimes Danny.' She finished and turned away and pushed her palms to both temples in frustration.

'God huh?' Danny asked. 'I don't think you should "God" me anymore ma. I've heard just about enough of God.'

His Mother turned back to face him again and ran her hands through her tangled hair. 'Enough of God, Danny? Really? What, you don't think he exists now?' She asked with a look of concern emerging on her face.

'I don't fucking know Ma. Maybe he does, maybe he doesn't. But if he does, he's asleep at the wheel half the time.'

'I don't like that kind of talk Danny. That's not how I raised you.' She said defiantly. 'What happened to having faith? I always thought there was strong faith inside you.'

Danny's shoulders softened as he leaned forward in the rocking chair and his head in his hands and his elbow's heavily on his knees. 'I'm sorry Ma. I guess all I'm saying is that sometimes . . . I feel like he's doing nothing . . . except sitting up there, wherever he is . . . Shooting arrows with his fucking eyes shut.'

His mother's face buckled in a frown. She looked to be on the brink of tears only unable to produce anymore. She turned to leave the room, but turned back abruptly and asked Danny bluntly, 'Why did you come here Danny? Why did you come home?'

Danny's gaze stayed towards the floor as he pondered the answer to her simple question. A simple question with a not so simple answer, not one at least that he would give her.

She shook her head disapprovingly, 'Nothing Danny? Well, at least tell me why you're here in my apartment then. There's plenty other places to go. Why are you here?'

Danny slowly raised his eyes to meet hers, suddenly looking quite young and quite old all at once. 'To sleep Mom. Really, I just wanted to sleep for a little while. Is that okay?'

'The couch is yours Danny.' She said leaving the living room. ''Stay as long as you want'.

30 BRENDAN'S ASSIGNMENT

Brendan sprawled out on his hotel bed at the Marriott in Quincy Center. He laid there with his hands clasped across his chest still fully dressed except for his feet. He had ditched the shoes in the middle of the floor at his feet, next to his packed suitcase, and found his way into the hotel's standard-issue room slippers.

The TV was on, but he had turned the volume down to zero. He preferred the sound of cars from the highway speeding in the distance and the hum of the central heating system to the repeated Cialis and Viagra commercials that ran on an endless loop on the History channel.

His face held a whisper of dark stubble since he

hadn't bothered to shave in the last 36 hours or so. 'At least I showered and changed my clothes' he thought. 'That was progress for someone cooped up nonstop in this asylum for what feels like eternity. It's like prison all over again, except for the maids of course who do nothing but look at me like I'm an eccentric, a modern day Thoreau or a fugitive hiding out . . . or some combination of both.' His patience had begun to fray after 24 hours of waiting for the phone call that may or may not arrive.

He couldn't help but chew on his fingernails while anticipating the details of the 'favor' that had been asked of him. He got to a point where there were no fingernails left and resorted to biting and picking at the skin on his fingertips, a terrible habit he'd developed at some stage recently.

The phone rang loudly all of a sudden and Brendan jumped at the sound of it. He'd expected the noise to come for so long, but he never wished that it would. The ringing caught him off guard so much that when he leapt up, he tripped over his scattered shoes in a panic to answer the phone.

He managed to answer finally by the 4th ring with a heavier breath than he expected. He breathed into the receiver, 'Hello?'

A familiar voice responded, 'Hey smart-guy, what disgusting habit has you so out of breath?'

'Ah . . . it's nothing.' He answered, 'I just tripped that's all, the phone ringing caught me by surprise.'

'Yeah? Well, glad I called. I feel like I would've had to do CPR on you if I'd decided to knock and you're really not my type. Listen junior, you know my voice right?'

'Um, yeah, it sounds familiar. It's Mc . . .' Brendan started.

'Don't! Fucking say my name guy are you shitting me.'

'Sorry, yeah of course.' Brendan had forgotten how charming and frightening his old prison pal McNulty could be.

'Now, Junior, what I want you to do is very simple.' McNulty continued, 'It's nothing dangerous and it's nothing illegal.'

'Good, okay, sounds good, I was worried for a while. What is it?' Brendan asked.

'I can't spell it out over the fucking phone guy. Put your fucking dress and high heels on and go check out at reception. There's a letter waiting for you behind the front desk. That'll lay out everything I need you to do.'

'What if there's questions or anything?' Brendan asked 'Can I contact you.'

'Don't worry there won't be and you most certainly cannot contact me.' McNulty answered. 'Listen . . . a retarded chimpanzee could do this thing for me, so I trust you can manage it also. Now . . . get your ass down there, pretty fucking please.'

Brendan heard the phone click softly as McNulty hung up. His mind filled with a crippling doubt at that moment. 'Redemption' he thought 'It's my one real chance at redemption.' With that thought he bent to put his shoes on and grabbed his case to move out. He caught a glimpse of his reflection in the mirror on his way out. He paused only briefly, just enough time to shrug to his own reflection. He headed out the door and pulled the key card from the light slot and let the heavy door slam shut behind him.

He waited until he was sitting in the back of a taxi out front of the hotel before he opened the envelope. When he did, he found a card inside with an address neatly printed on it along with a small torn piece of paper with the following note scribbled on it in messy handwriting:

Junior - Let Dora know your plans for tonight. You're meeting friends at Mackin's Saloon in Quincy

Center. Make sure she relays your plans to her brother. Then get your ass on a fucking train back to Philly.

Brendan stuck the address card in his pocket. He crumbled the note in his hand, then popped it in his mouth and chewed quickly. Still chewing, he caught the taxi driver's eyes in the rearview mirror. He gave him a confident nod and said, 'head towards Dorchester, I'll show you where to drop me.

31 DANNY ON THE MOVE

Danny woke to the familiar sound of metal grating the pavement. He knew right away it must have snowed at least lightly while he slept. 'Enough to have someone's pick-up truck scraping a snow plow on the ground' he thought, as he blinked his eyes open.

He had expected to dream. He always dreamt. Even long days at work made him dream. He'd fall asleep and be right back in a conference room arguing over the company's risk appetite or some other mundane topic. So when he shut his eyes only to blink them open in what seemed like a second later, he didn't feel refreshed. He didn't feel like he'd slept at all. He wasn't alert or rested or any different at all from when he'd first laid down. 'Maybe slightly less of a headache' he thought, 'but just barely. Time must have past however since it was pitch dark out and not a sound could be heard in the house. He searched for words to describe how he felt as he laid there staring at fringes of light from beyond the cracks in the window shades. It wasn't day light that split through, 'too late for that this time of year. It must be a street light just outside the apartment. That must be hell, sleeping with that burning flame in your periphery each evening.' He tried to think of the right adjective to describe his mental state, but he couldn't put his finger on it. His mind grasped at his rusty vocabulary, 'trapped, stuck, down in a hole, stuck in the middle, boxed in, boxed out, boxed off, punched out, cornered, back against the wall, backed into a corner, standing in cement, standing in glue, on an island, up shit's creek, no paddle, gone, forgotten, gone and forgotten, hesitant, paused, procrastination, frozen, scared stiff, frankensteined, stutter-stepped . . . Just fucking lost. . . driven to inaction.'

He sat up quickly and inadvertently kicked the blanket to the ground as he swung his legs around to plant his feet on the carpet. As he stood up he heard the floor boards underneath him creek, 'better the floor than my knees' he thought. He walked slowly across the dark living room into the darker hallway. It felt much later than it was and he felt childish all of a sudden and just plain dumb when he realized he had been tip-toeing like it was Christmas morning. There was no one there to wake up. When he flicked on the kitchen light, the note on the refrigerator confirmed his suspicions that his Mother had gone out.

The note was brief and written in a familiar scribble. It read, 'Had to run some errands, help yourself to any food. Sorry, but needed my car. Love Mom.'

Danny opened the fridge to find a plate of dinner made for him and covered in plastic wrap. He thought better of eating it, 'stomach might react badly to a healthy meal'. Plus, he needed to get moving. He kicked himself about the car. He thought he'd have no problem borrowing it and had assumed it to be his main mode of transport. Instead he rifled through a pen jar for train fare. He grabbed his toothbrush from the duffle bag and brushed his teeth in the bathroom. He winced at the strong cinnamon flavored toothpaste, which was the same shiny red tube he hated as a kid. He found some blue Listerine under the sink which he gargled with for a minute to wash the remnants of the red poison from his mouth.

He changed into a dark sweater and warmer shoes, then grabbed a black winter hat and his leather gloves from his bag. On his way out he found the spare key hanging on a hook near the door and stuffed it into his pocket just before he pulled the door closed tightly behind him.

The streets were cleared but there was a good dusting of fresh powder on the sidewalks, about 2-3 inches thick. The snow was light however and easily kicked away, 'too cold to snow heavily' he thought and peered into the glare of the streetlight to judge how hard the snow was falling. It was the same method he and Jim used as kids. They would always take shifts watching around the glow of the streetlights, elbows on the window sill, hoping to see fast-falling, heavy white crystals that meant a likely day off from school. This time however, he saw barely anything as the snow that started earlier tapered off to an occasional flurry. The childhood memory rekindled a practiced pain in his chest. 'Not so much a pain' he thought, 'as a dead weight'. Sorrow and guilt gripped him each time he remembered moments with his younger brother, which was often. The ghost of Jim Carson walked next to him on most nights and this one was no different. He half expected to see parallel footsteps matching closely to his own in the fresh powder. He stopped at the edge of the curb and peered down at his feet. He looked quickly behind him to his left, then to his right focusing on the untouched snow lying motionless on the sidewalk. Reassured of his sanity, he shivered as he tried to chase the thoughts away from his mind. He continued on and stepped into the street. He crossed carefully as several stalled construction works made it more precarious than necessary. He leapt over a large pot hole to avoid the splatter of its contents that included dirt encrusted ice water. He high stepped over the tall temporary curb. Safely across the street, he started over the hill past a couple of low budget chain restaurants and past the old high school on his left. At the school crosswalk, he sped up to a jog towards a drive-through parking lot with a side passage to the train station. He heard a prolonged horn sound behind him and turned back to see a dark hooded figure make a hand motion to the beeping driver and continue at pace in the same direction as himself. Although dressed in black on a dark night, Danny could still make out a sizable frame underneath the man's clothing. Under the street light the figure cast an eclipsing shadow and it moved with an easy agility that defied its size.

Danny pulled his gloves tighter onto his hands out of habit and flexed his fists to stretch the leather to form. He tugged his hat down lower to cover the bottom of his ears which had become exposed during his trot across the street. He cut through the side passage way that led into the train station's commuter parking lot. He quickened his pace towards the back steps and took the stairs with speed two at a time. Pushing his way through the cold and huddled crowd that was waiting on buses in droves, he slipped through the swinging doors into the train station. He pulled his right glove off to dig out his coins and popped the change into the ticket machine. He waited for the Charlie card to spit out and grabbed it quickly as it did. He shot through the barrier as he heard the sound of a train approaching the platform. The doors opened just as he reached the bottom step and he walked onto the first car. The empty train brought relief as he didn't have to hustle for a chair. He felt weak suddenly and had hoped for a seat and some personal space.

He walked to the end of the car and grabbed an empty two-seater for himself, spreading out to deter any potential neighbors. When he heard the beeping sound that precedes the doors closing, he shut his eyes in quiet relief and exhaled slowly a breath he only just realized he'd been holding. The doors started to close, but a loud thump of the brakes indicated that someone made the jump just in time. The doors opened again slowly, then slammed shut within seconds. Danny sensed the heat of human presence and opened his eyes to see a beastly sized man dressed in all black take the empty seat directly across from him. Danny's eyes followed the figure from his wet work boots, past his tight peacoat and up to his face.

His mind cleared as he saw a familiar face and he laughed gently to himself in mild disbelief. Danny felt a flood of forgotten memories from long ago as he continued to stare directly into McNulty's eyes.

McNulty was first to break the silence and asked quietly 'You believe in coincidences Dan?'

Danny's slight smile faded with his answer, as he felt a rush of rage building, 'Fucking Bullshit. Let me guess, of all the gin joints in all the world, right McNulty?'

McNulty shrugged his shoulders guiltily, 'I see you still have trust issues Danny. I'd hoped you grow out of that.'

Danny coughed a laugh with disgust, 'Oh . . . don't get me wrong, I trust plenty of people McNulty, just not you or anyone else even loosely affiliated with my old man. You should know that.'

McNulty shook his head disapprovingly, 'You shouldn't harbor ill will Danny, it'll eat you alive from the inside out. You may not like me or trust me, but I'm old enough and bad enough to be damn certain of that.'

Danny coughed into his hand and rubbed the day-old stubble on his chin. He pulled the tight wool hat from his head leaving his hair in disarray. 'Alright McNulty' he said and leaned his elbows to his knees to draw him closer into the conversation. 'I didn't wake up this morning to bicker with some of my father's old homeboys . . . so I'm sorry okay, my bad.'

'Likewise Dan' McNulty answered and leant back into his seat. 'I meant no disrespect either, I'm sure I caught you by surprise.'

'Yeah I guess you did' Danny answered 'So maybe now you'll tell me then huh?'

'What's that?' McNulty asked, trying his best to look confused.

'Listen man, we both know this was no chance encounter. I'm not that unlucky. Sift through the bullshit man and tell me. It was you following me and doing a pretty bad job of it. I'll admit you move well for a man of your . . . girth, but not the most subtle approach now is it?'

McNulty chuckled in what seemed like agreement. 'Following you . . . maybe, but not in the way you think Danny. I heard you were back, so I came by to say hello. I saw you in the distance.' You have the same angry strut as your old man, so I knew it was you. So I tried to run and catch up to you.'

Danny was skeptical by nature and already decided whatever McNulty said was going to be a fairy tale, but he decided not to push it too much. 'You heard I was back huh? Sure you did, news must have travelled fast then.'

'We're in a new world kid' McNulty replied. 'News is instant and endless if you ask me.'

'Whatever' Danny said, 'anyway you're here now, what is it you wanted to say to me?'

'Just one question really . . . and one simple request, that's all.'

'Okay then' Danny answered, relieved with what he hoped would turn into directness. 'Ask your question, then we'll see about that request.'

'Simple Dan. Why are you here?' McNulty asked

Danny's face scrunched into confusion. 'What . . . I can't visit my home now?'

'Visits are planned and vacations typically last longer than 3 days Danny. 72 hours is just enough time to get into some serious trouble.'

'You're certainly well researched, I'll give you that McNulty. Now how you got my itinerary I'm not even going to ask because I don't think I want to know the answer. Regardless, I wouldn't worry your head about me and trouble. I'm not here for trouble.'

'Well now it's me not trusting you Danny boy. Funny isn't it?' McNulty said as he stood up slowly, holding onto the pole for support. The train began to slow as it approached Quincy Center station. Anyway, Danny, good seeing you, but I gotta date to meet an old friend so this is my stop.' He walked over and with a head nod turned to look out the door.

Danny sat still, confused with the whole conversation. He asked, 'Hey McNulty. I never heard your request. Let's have it.'

McNulty turned back as the doors opened 'Oh right' he said 'I forgot. It's an easy one Danny. There's nothing but badness here for you now boy. My request . . . is that you go home. And do it soon.'

'I am home' Danny said 'Did you forget that?'

McNulty stepped out off the train, but turned back to Danny from the edge of the platform. 'Not no more kid. Your home's 3,000 miles east, on a small, moss-colored island in the Atlantic. Take it from me, go there and try to get your life back.'

The doors closed then and as the train slowly chugged away from the platform Danny watched McNulty. He watched him stand there very still with a waved hand in the air until he finally faded from sight. Danny sat back into the chair and put his hat back on tightly. He breathed in and out deeply and drifted into a dreamlike trance pondering just what meeting McNulty meant. He shut his eyes and rested in the comfort that even if he fell asleep, Braintree was the last stop on the Redline.

32 BRENDAN AND DORA

Brendan walked around in Dorchester Park for the better part of an hour. He was trying to muster up the courage to face Dora, someone he once felt so strongly for . . . and possibly he'd even face Flynn, someone who routinely crippled him with fear. There was always the chance that Flynn could be just around the corner, waiting to pounce on him.

In the large, woodsy park in the middle of Dorchester, he had started out by sitting on a bench near the kids' playground, but when people started to realize he was alone and not with any of the children playing, he sensed their apprehension and felt it was time to move on. He strolled aimlessly for a time through the tarmacked trails and stood for a while at the top of a hill overlooking the baseball diamond.

As it grew dark and began to flurry, the silent woods began to haunt him and he headed out of the park down a side pathway towards the dim streetlights on Richmond Street. At the bottom of the lane way, he took a right and walked the 50 yards or so to the address he'd been given from McNulty. He thought about how if things had turned out differently, much differently, he could have been quite familiar with this address.

He thought longingly about Dora as he loitered across the street from her apartment, trying to be as nonchalant as possible. The shades were drawn but there were lights on and he was certain that the flickering he saw belonged to the television. He gathered himself after a minute of mental preparation and headed across the street. Ascending her steps he knew this was not going to run as smoothly as he'd hoped. He could just feel it. Before he even reached the landing he heard movement from the inside and a porch light came on followed immediately by a door opening.

Brendan froze, and for a second he nearly toppled over in surprise, completely caught on the back foot.

He hadn't expected even an answer to his knock at the door, never mind a pre-emptive strike. As his eyes adjusted to the light, he saw her silhouette emerge from the doorway.

'Can I help you with something? Dora asked, trying to hide that she was clearly startled herself by a stranger lingering outside of her apartment. 'I saw you across the street, what are you some kind of pervert?' She held up her phone and said, 'All I need to do is hit 'talk' and the cops will be on the way.'

'You don't need to do that Dora.' Brendan said, after regaining his footing.

The use of her name seemed to startle Dora again, but this time only momentarily because of its familiarity. 'I know that voice' she said as she edged slowly onto the porch from the door threshold to peer closer.

Brendan finally took another step forward, entering the landing of the porch. When he did, the light shone bright on his face, unmasking him to Dora's eyes.

He shielded the blast of light from his own eyes and noticed Dora take a step back into the doorway to steady herself. Brendan paused, momentarily at a loss for how to proceed. He half raised his hand in a wave, but thought it awkward and inappropriate as he cut himself off in mid motion.

Dora grabbed the door quickly and Brendan panicked as his opportunity to speak drew dangerously to a close. 'Wait! Please.' He said more forcefully than he'd intended.

Dora stopped from closing the door, but stayed huddled next to it, still poised to shut it fast if necessary. 'I'm just here to talk Dora' Brendan pleaded 'that's all. Please.' His tone had adjusted to a gentler one.

'Well I've got nothing to say to you, and I'm even less interested in hearing you out.' Dora replied.

'But, that's why I'm here' Brendan answered then paused, frantically thinking of what to say next as the speech he semi-prepared for this encounter fell from his memory. 'I came here to clear the air with you . . . and your brother.'

Dora laughed suddenly, a mean laugh, 'You think Flynn's ever gonna forget about you?' she asked rhetorically, 'Jesus Brendan, you've got no clue. I . . . I think . . . you should just go.' She said, then she moved to shut the door for definite this time.

Brendan reacted instantly and stuck his foot in the

doorway just in time to prevent the door from slamming to a close. The door popped aggressively off the rubber from his sneaker and caught Dora by surprise. She stumbled backwards into her living room.

Brendan lurched forward and grabbed her before she could fall over. He had reacted from instinct so quickly that before he knew what he was doing he found himself standing close to her, holding firmly onto her arms, their faces barely inches apart.

They stood silently for a moment that felt much longer than it was. Her eyes, which at first showed fear, relaxed and he watched her pupils dilate, eyes shining bright blue before his own. He had forgotten how attractive her eyes could be when they smiled and how beautiful she was when her shiny red strands of hair draped the edges of her cheeks. He inched closer to her face with his own and pulled her arms closer to him. As he did, he felt her arms tense at first, but then relax slightly as she slid her wrists and forearms around his waist and she moved her lips the final inch to press against his own.

....

Afterwards Brendan didn't dare drift off to sleep.

He laid on his side and gently rubbed her bare shoulder as he watched her eyes struggle to remain open, eventually giving in to the urge to close completely.

Brendan wrestled with his thoughts as he tried to figure out his next move. His stomach ached with butterflies and he felt at any second he could vomit. Things had not gone as planned, not even slightly. This had just happened. He couldn't articulate how he felt. He obviously still loved her and he guessed she still felt something for him. He hoped she did at least. However, it was difficult to fight back logic, no matter how hard he tried. 'Anyway that this shakes out' he thought, 'it does not end up with a future for us.'

He reached down to the floor and into the pocket of his crumbled jeans and pulled out his watch, startled to see nearly 2 hours had past already. Decision time was upon him and he knew it. He slowly lifted the covers off himself and slid his legs out from the bed. As he pulled his jeans on, he heard Dora move and turned towards her as she asked, 'Where are you heading so soon?'

Brendan knelt back on the bed and leant over to kiss her. 'Just to the kitchen' He answered 'Need a drink, don't worry. Stay there. I'll bring you some water.'

'Okay' she answered and shifted to her other side in the bed. The blankets slipped down her shoulder and Brendan winced in physical pain at seeing how beautiful her white porcelain skin looked next to the shine of her hair. He knew he had to leave now or he would never again have the strength to do so. 'It's like pulling off a band-aid' he thought.

He silently lifted his shirt and sneakers from the floor as he left the room. He put his clothes back on in the living room quickly and quietly. He went to the kitchen sink and ran the faucet. Meanwhile he found a pen and pad of paper in the utensil draw. He began to scribble down his note to Dora, knowing full well that any attempt at an apology would sound merely empty or worse, callous.

He kept the note brief, ending with a reassurance that he meant to make amends with her and Flynn and carefully noted his plans to meet some people that night at Mackin's pub in Quincy Center. Feeling as empty as his written words, Brendan slipped out the front door and started off briskly down Richmond Street towards Adams Street. He began in a walk that quickly went into a jog, then a flat out run, stopping only about a mile later at the old chocolate factory where he took the steps down to the trolley station at the Milton Stop to wait for his train.

'Running again' he thought as he tried in vain to catch his breath, 'always running'.

33 FLYNN'S APOLOGY

The prison psychiatrist once told Flynn of a theory that basically, in his understanding, amounted to drug and alcohol abuse during early adolescence can stunt your emotional growth. She said that in one breath and in the next told him that it didn't mean he could use that to rationalize his actions. She had said it so that he could recognize a shortcoming in himself and start to use that knowledge to try and control his urges.

Logically he understood it because it made sense. Obviously filling your body full of chemicals and killing off brain cells from an early age had a negative effect on you. Later when he thought more about it, he decided he definitely believed it. There were many things he had done in his life that he now wished he'd done differently. Not just the obvious big things, but also the small things he had done, to people he loved that he never before thought twice about. How many times had he blown up at Dora for little to no reason, leaving her a nervous wreck half of the time. When he thought about it, she was really the only family to him that mattered, probably the only person he had any significant connection to in his life. He thought about how often she had covered for him, taken care of him, protected him in a way. He had never said thank you, and never even showed the slightest hint of appreciation. He just continued on doing what he does, stirring up trouble and leaving her to deal with the consequences. 'I was gone for 2 years, who else did she have?' he thought, 'no wonder she had tried reconnecting to our mother, with me as a brother and a drunk and distant father. How could I blame her?'

He had been pondering all this and more while sitting on the tailgate of his truck, chain-smoking and watching airplanes fly overhead at Castle Island. Even if it was in the middle of Southie and was always packed with people, there was something relaxing about the place. Fort Independence, which was perched on a hill overlooking Boston Harbor now comfortably served as a picnic area and playground for the city's youth.

After the argument with Dora, he drove his old truck around aimlessly for a while until economic realities set in and he needed to stop burning through his gas since it was needed for the work week. The rage he felt leaving Dora's apartment subsided with time. As was the usual case, immense guilt set in shortly thereafter. Guilt was how he operated. Usually, he turned guilt away from himself into anger at those who he felt guilty about. Strangely this time however, he felt he couldn't do that. Not to Dora, not anymore. When it became too dark to see the planes land anymore, he grabbed a couple of hotdogs from Sully's, the burger and ice cream institution on Castle Island and had them both ingested before he reached Morissey Boulevard leading to Dorchester. He stopped at the florist across from Cedar Grove cemetery and was able to pick up a bouquet of flowers just before they closed for the night.

He drove around the corner and parked, blocking the driveway to Dora's apartment minutes later. He felt like she had to be home, but there seem to be no lights on that he could see. There was an eerie darkness to the street that night as it seemed all the street lights were enveloped by red, yellow and brown leaves. Flynn shivered when he opened the door, realizing the temperature dropped significantly with the transition to darkness.

He walked tenderly up the porch stairs, sliding the light covering of snow off the edges of the steps with his boot. He rang the doorbell and waited patiently for a response. After a minute, he rang the bell again. He thought maybe she had actually gone out, but part of him just knew she was there. He opened the screen door and tried the knob to the main door and found it opened. He walked in slowly, knocking on the door again as he did so and gently called Dora's name. The lights were off in the living room and kitchen. He saw an old glass vase on top of the refrigerator and got it down. He ran the kitchen sink and rinsed out the vase. As he did, he noticed a note scribbled on a loose piece of paper on the counter. He read the note carefully. Any other day of his life, he knew it would've driven him to rage. Today for some reason, he felt only sorrow. It could've been the smudged ink from what looked like painful tears touching the parchment. He put the note down carefully where it had been before and filled the vase up with lukewarm water. He cut the flower stems at an angle with a pair of scissors from the fork draw and put them into the water.

He noticed as he turned, a dim light came on in Dora's bedroom. He walked back through the living room and knocked lightly on the bedroom door. The door opened slightly with the weight of his fist. 'Dora?' he called again and pushed through the door slowly. 'You okay?'

He felt his own eyes well up in tears when he saw Dora. She sat on the edge of the bed next to the lamp on the bedside table. Her red hair covered her hands, which in turn covered her eyes. He walked slowly towards her and knelt down slowly in front of her, bending his head low to try and get a look through her hands to her face.

She removed her hands finally and dragged her hair back behind her ears. Flynn noticed the edges of her red hair were darker than the rest, wet with tears. Her eye's, though bright blue were rubbed red around the edges and they matched the red from her nose that also gave away that she'd been crying. She didn't speak at all. Flynn had rarely seen her in such a state, if ever. He always thought of her as the toughest girl he knew, and she was, which made it all the more painful to watch her now. 'I'm sorry' he said. 'For everything I mean, not just today. I love you, I've never actually told you that . . . and you're all the family I've got. I promise, from now on, things'll be different. I mean it. You may not believe me right now, but they will.'

Dora just nodded in agreement. After a period of silence she answered, 'I love him Flynn. You need to fix this.'

Flynn felt his eyes grow heavy with water again. 'I know' he responded 'I will fix it. I read the letter. I'm going now.' He squeezed her knee, and she put a hand over his, as he got up from the carpet. Neither of them said anything else. Flynn walked slowly from her room and through the living room to the front door. He closed the door behind him when he left, making sure the lock caught this time. He started his truck and wiped his eyes dry with his sleeves. Driving away, he thought about how for the first time really in his life, he was going to do something for someone other than himself and he felt good about it. It was like a small weight from a big pile had just been removed from his chest.

34 FLYNN MEETS MCNULTY

Flynn pulled up the hill and swung the old truck into the bumpy dirt parking lot behind Mackin's Saloon. He knew what he had to do and he knew why, but the thought of entering a bar room made him nervous. Since his parole, he'd managed to stay clean, but not without significant mental effort on his part. One way to stay off booze and drugs was to stay out of the places where they existed. He kept out of bars and he'd kept as far away as possible from anyone from his past drug exploits. He got out of the truck and shut the door hard to make sure it would stay closed. He felt like gravity was heavier than normal. His legs moved sluggishly with the strain of his long emotional day.

The parking lot was emptier than he'd expected,

'especially for a place that was supposed to be hosting a party' He thought. 'Maybe I'm early.' He swallowed a gulp of saliva and took a deep breath outside the front door. He hoped he wouldn't see too many people from his past sitting inside the local bar room. After a final moment of deliberation, he turned, put his head down and walked through the heavy wooden door.

Inside was slightly brighter than the dark street outside. The bar looked the same as he remembered. It was still one of the few popular bar rooms in Quincy that looked like a local boozer instead of one refurbished to look like a night club. He recognized the female bartender, but couldn't remember her name. He didn't recognize the man sitting on a stool next to the front door, presumably checking ID's. No one asked him for anything as he walked in.

He went over to the bar while he scanned the rest of the room. The new juke box was playing, but there was no one else in the bar at all, the place was flat out empty. He felt awkward and out of place when he realized he was the only there not on the payroll.

He thought, 'The music playing on the juke box was good and the television had Sportscenter on, so it could be worse.' He sat down at a table close to the bar. The bartender looked up and said 'Hello, what are you having?'

Flynn paused. He actually hadn't thought about what he'd do when he was asked for a drink. He hadn't planned a response or thought of an alternative. He responded out of habit more so than anything else and said 'Bud light draft'. She rang him up and he paid her and left a dollar on the counter for a tip. He put the beer in the middle of the table and leaned his chin on his hands to stare at the condensation dripping down the cold glass. In his head he knew he didn't even want the beer, but now that it sat in front of him, it was calling for him. He continued staring at the full glass for over a minute. His concentration was so great he hadn't realized a very large man dressed in black come out from the bathroom and take a seat at the bar only an arms-length away from him.

It wasn't until the man got up from the bar stool and sat across from Flynn at the table that Flynn shook free from the hypnotic suds. He looked up at the man's face and thought he was pretty familiar, although he felt he would've remembered clearly any man with shoulders that broad and square, so he must not know him. He was confused about why the man had just taken a seat across from him, at his table, with not one other patron present in the bar. Flynn didn't scare easy however, and broad shoulders be damned, he would not be intimidated. He looked the man in the eye, but decided to let him speak first.

After a minute of non-verbal posturing, the large man broke his eye contact and showed a small smile. 'You like the Matrix?' he asked.

Flynn scrunched his eyebrows in confusion and replied, 'What? The fucking movie with Keanu Reeves?'

'Yeah. That's the one. You like it?'

'I guess it's alright.' Flynn answered still confused. 'Any reason? Or is that how you start all conversations with total strangers.'

'You were staring at that beer so hard I was waiting for the thing to bend like the spoon in the movie, that's all. Plus we're two Quincy guys in Mackin's. We haven't met before, but we sure ain't strangers.'

'How do you know I'm from Quincy?' Flynn asked.

'You're in Mackin's and you don't have an Irish accent, where the fuck else would you be from?'

Flynn laughed at the man's response and decided

he must just be old and lonely, here looking to socialize with the only other person in the place. 'Okay then, you got me. I'm a Quincy guy. My name's Flynn.' Flynn reached around his beer glass across the table to shake hands with his new acquaintance. 'Nice to meet you man.'

'Nice to meet you too Flynn' the man replied. 'I'm McNulty, Nick McNulty. Friends call me Nicky. Everyone else calls me McNulty.'

'What should I call you?' Flynn asked.

'How about Nick? You can call me Nick. Sound like a good compromise?'

'Sure does Nick.' Flynn answered. 'So . . . um . . . what brings you out tonight?'

'Isn't it obvious Flynn? I came out to meet some ladies.'

Flynn laughed again and thought he was really starting to like this guy.

'What about you?' McNulty asked. 'You're clearly not here to drink that beer, that's for certain.' McNulty pointed to Flynn's beer, which had become warm and flat in the brief time that they spoke.

'No' Flynn responded. 'Not here for the beer, not sure why I even ordered it. I guess old habits die hard. I'm hoping to meet someone here that's all. Need to talk to someone and clear something up for my sister. The guy's supposed to be in here tonight.'

'Sounds ominous my young companion, should I expect trouble?'

'No, no, not from me, I'm here to squash something not start something.' Flynn answered.

'Good' McNulty said 'I cower at the thought of physical violence.'

Flynn gave him a funny look accompanied with a smirk, 'I would've guessed otherwise Nick.'

'Well, appearances are not always as they seem, but perhaps I exaggerated a little.' McNulty answered. 'So is it 'One Day at a Time' then Flynn? You're in the program I take it?'

'What, AA? Um, yeah I guess I kinda am.'

'Sounds more complicated than that' McNulty said. 'Then again, it's usually something complicated, self-inflicted or otherwise that sends people to those meetings. It definitely ain't the coffee, that's for sure. Donuts maybe, but the coffee's consistently shit.'

Flynn laughed and asked, 'So are you in AA too then? Pretty shit luck for this bar huh? Only two people in the place, both are off the fucking sauce.'

McNulty laughed heartily, 'Good point Flynn, tough break for this place. I'm in the program. Well, sort of in the program. I dip in and dip out, been doing so for about 30 years.'

'Doesn't sound too successful, sorry to hear that. What's your poison, if you don't mind me asking, is it booze or drugs?'

'Geez Flynn, don't even buy me dinner first huh?'

'Sorry man, I shouldn't have asked that. My bad.'

'No it's okay Flynn. I get it, you're new to this and you want to learn that's good. Truth is, for me it's neither. My involvement is more what you'd call . . . State imposed.'

'Oh. Okay, well if it makes you feel better Nick, you're in good company.'

'Young man like you, sorry to hear that Flynn. What'd you do time for?' McNulty asked.

'I . . . ahh . . . I don't think I want to talk about that actually. It was . . . not my finest moment and I don't want to relive it.'

'So you were guilty I take it?' McNulty asked.

'Yeah man. I was guilty alright . . . I still am.' Flynn answered. He reached over and put his hand around his beer. He lifted it up and looked into the glass, trying to catch his reflection in the liquid, but seeing only a distorted picture of McNulty's face across the table. He pushed his chair back and got up. He walked the couple steps over to the bar and handed the beer back to the bartender and asked for a coke instead. When he turned back around to take his chair again, he saw McNulty smile and give him a mock golf-clap.

'Fuck it, right Nick? Who needs it?'

McNulty nodded in agreement. 'That's willpower young Flynn, very impressive.'

'Thanks' Flynn replied

McNulty leaned forward on the table and rubbed his chin with his hand. 'A lot of things been done through willpower, amazing things, shit people thought impossible. You want to hear a quick story about willpower Flynn?'

'Ah yeah man, I'm here anyway, got nothing but time.' Flynn answered.

'Good . . . when I was about your age, there was this bad motherfucker that ran a lot of the drugs through Dorchester, Quincy and the South Shore. Let's call him Jack. He wasn't the top guy or anything, but he had some weight locally. And, he loved to throw that weight around whenever possible. He loved fucking with average Joe's. It made him feel hard or something. I hated the fucking asshole. But, I didn't need to worry about him, ya know. I wasn't on anything and no one I hung with was either, so no need. A very close friend of mine however had a different situation. He was pretty straight edge himself, had two kids, head screwed on straight. He used to work for me in a shop I used to run back in the day. He had balls this guy and he was tough as nails, but most of all, anything he wanted, he went after it. He had willpower like no one I'd ever seen.

One night, my friend's two younger brothers wound up at a party with some of the wrong people, including Jack. The youngest brother apparently made a misguided pass at the wrong woman. A young chick who the dealer had a little crush on. Problem was, she didn't feel the same about him, but she did show interest in my friend's brother. Jack got jealous. Jack didn't like being jealous. So when my buddy's other brother asked Jack to set him up with an eight ball, Jack did it, but he spiked it heavy with something like rat poison. My buddy's youngest brother was talked into doing the first line by Jack himself. He gave it to him as a taster for free because it was his first time. That one time was all it took. That hot shot took hold within seconds. My friend and I were only minutes away, but it didn't matter. John was gone before he got to Carney hospital.'

McNulty paused from his story and walked up to

the bar and got a glass of ice water. When the bartender handed it to him, he took a long gulp and then sat back down in the chair.

Flynn looked over at him questioningly 'So? What happened next man? What about your boy with the willpower, what did he do?'

McNulty smiled. 'What would you have done Flynn? Some motherfucker takes your younger brother's life away out of childish jealousy, what do you think? How does that end? How do you get him back?'

Flynn sat back in his chair. 'Shit. I don't know man. I guess . . . I mean, I don't have a brother or nothing, but I think I'd kill the motherfucker and anyone who tried to get in my way.' Flynn said emphatically.

'Yes! Young Flynn, you read my mind.' McNulty answered. 'And you're damn right too. My friend was an average Joe, just like any other hard working stiff. But, you know what he did? He walked right into that house, no weapons, no nothing and cleaned that place out. He fought through at least five guys, five grown men, paid to guard this fucker, with weapons and all. I know this for a fact, because I was there with him. Then he dragged Jack to the roof of the triple decker and threw the bastard off it. That . . . I also witnessed.'

'Shit man' Flynn said in response. 'Was he caught? I mean, did the police catch him?'

'Police? Nah, not then. He burned that house to the ground though, so wasn't much linking him to the scene. He sacrificed a lot though that night. From that point on, he was a ghost. Never around for more than a month at a time, cause someone or something was always after him. Plus he blamed himself for what happened to his brother. He blamed himself for not being there. The only thing he could do to dull the pain was to drown it in whiskey. And with that, the Ghost lost everything.'

'Fuck' Flynn said.

'Yeah. Fuck is right. The real victims though, unfortunately were the Carson boys. Those poor kids had to grow up with either their old man absent or drunk. Something I wish I never had to see.'

At the mention of the name Carson, Flynn slipped his foot off the bottom part of his chair and lurched forward knocking McNulty's water to the ground. 'Shit. Ahh . . . sorry Nick. I must've slipped.'

McNulty watched the water drip onto the ground, then looked coolly back at Flynn and smiled.

Flynn found the smile empty of humor and all of a

sudden felt sick with nerves. He decided to take a walk outside and get some air. 'Hey, excuse me a minute Nick. I'm going to head out front and have a smoke. I'll be back in and I'll get that water cleaned up.'

McNulty shrugged and remained seated and continued looking unflinchingly at Flynn. Flynn practically ran out of the bar and stopped short out front and took a deep breath of cold air that burned his lungs. 'Carson' he thought 'How can that be?'

He took his cigarettes out from his pocket and put one to his lips. He pulled his lighter up to light the smoke but it blew out with the wind. He hugged the side of the building to obstruct the wind from the flame. He turned up toward the hill and looked up to see a familiar car that he placed right away. It was the same 80's style Buick he'd seen parked next to his truck much earlier in the day. 'Was that today' he thought 'Can that be a coincidence? No fucking way.'

Despite his fear, he slowly walked towards the parked Buick trying to see through the tint whether there was anyone inside of it. He approached it cautiously, and leaned closer to see into the window. As he leaned forward, the passenger door shot open and a man jumped out quickly. The man looked mean and experienced. He was older, 50's or so, with slicked back hair and a salt and pepper goatee. He looked directly at Flynn, then pointed behind him.

Flynn turned quickly around to see the massive frame of McNulty shadowing the light from the main street. He looked down at McNulty's hand and followed it until he saw the glimmer flash off the chrome gun. His eyes opened with fright as he looked into McNulty's. McNulty just pointed to the Buick and said, 'Get in the fucking car Flynn.' Flynn had no choice. With trepidation, Flynn opened the back door to the car and slid across into the seat.

35 DANNY'S RECKONING

Danny's walk from the Braintree train station to Mike's house was short, but it was cold. The snow had stopped, but when it did the temperature dropped significantly. It had been years since he'd seen Mike's wife and kids. Even before Jim died, Danny hadn't taken much time on his trips home to visit the Riordan's.

He rang the doorbell and shivered on the front porch as he waited for an answer. From the porch, it looked like every light was on in the house and he could hear a commotion inside that sounded like little girls arguing. Danny saw a silhouette through the lace curtain covering the glass door. It was too petit to be Mike and when the door opened, Danny was greeted by Mike's wife Elaine. He hadn't seen her in what felt like a lifetime, but she still looked the same, like she hadn't aged at all. She looked to him like motherhood really suited her.

She smiled at him when she opened the door to let him in. 'Danny' she said affectionately. 'Wow, it feels like forever.' She pulled him into a hug and gave him a kiss on the cheek. 'Get inside Danny, it's freezing'.

'Hi Elaine, good to see you, thanks for having me over.' Danny said as he kissed her back on the cheek and walked into the hallway. He took off his hat and pulled off his gloves and stuffed them in his coat pocket. He looked around the house as he unzipped his coat and draped it over the bannister at the bottom of the stairs. Nothing in the house looked familiar to him. Not just that he hadn't been in there really since the kids were babies, but also that the lifestyle was so foreign to him as well. He felt weak and alone all of sudden, confronted with a life that he had once envisioned for himself, but never achieved.

Elaine appeared to notice his silence and took it as something else, 'Sorry Danny, the place is a mess. The girls leave toys everywhere.'

Danny turned to her and smiled. 'No, it's perfect, sorry for staring. Just looks so different since I was last around. I . . . um . . . I'm sorry I wasn't around more. I should've visited more often.' He apologized.

'You still can. We're not going anywhere Danny. You can visit whenever you'd like.' She answered. Here, come on in, Mike was fixing something out back. Head through the hall there to the kitchen, he should be back in shortly.' She led him in and pointed through the long hall to the kitchen.

Danny nodded in thanks and walked through the hall towards the back of the house. He walked past the living room and saw the two girls and smiled and said 'Hello'. Both little girls went silent, but stared closely at Danny not sure who or what he was.

'Don't be rude girls. Say hi to your cousin Danny!' Danny heard Mike yell from the back door as he walked into the kitchen. Danny was happy with the intrusion as it broke the awkward silence between him and the children. He walked into the kitchen and saw Mike shut the door and stamp his boots on the door mat before walking in. 'Danny boy' he said. 'Long time no see'. He walked over and the two men shook hands. 'You want a beer or something?' He asked as he took his coat off and hung on a hook next to the door.

Danny considered the offer for a second before answering. 'You got anything stronger lying around

Mike?'

'Sit down' Mike said, 'I'll sort you out.' He reached up to the top cabinet and pulled down two whiskey glasses, then went over to a tall liquor cabinet and took down a bottle of 12 year old Jameson. 'This more like it?' he asked

'Yes. It is.' Danny answered and took a seat at a counter stool.

Mike poured two glasses, filling both more than halfway with the whiskey. He brought the glasses over to the counter and handed one to Danny. He put the other glass down, then walked over to get the bottle and took it over with him to the counter and put it down between the two glasses. Mike then sat down across from Danny and wrapped both hands around the drink.

Danny looked at Mike's large builder hands, then back up to his eyes. 'So, you learned how to sip the whiskey after all huh?' He said trying to smile.

Mike nodded slowly and also attempted a smile. 'I'm not in so much of a rush when I'm home already, ya know?'

'I guess you're right.' Danny answered. 'Elaine . . . she still looks great' he said awkwardly. 'And, the uh girls, they got big.'

'Thanks Dan. Yeah, it's been a while man. The girls'll be teenagers before I know it. I'll be chasing boys and shit away from the house I'm sure. Not looking forward to that one bit.'

Danny laughed. 'I think you've got a few years until that happens. Better stay sharp though just in case. You don't want to be shown up by some young punk.'

'I think we both know that ain't happening on my watch.' Mike answered. 'When the time comes, I'll be ready.'

'No, I think you're right. I think you have the intimidation factor down alright.'

Danny saw Elaine lean into the kitchen out of the corner of his eye. 'Mike' she said 'I'm going to get the girls down and probably head to bed myself. I'll let you boys catch up. Don't fly off without saying goodbye Danny.' She said and blew them both a kiss goodnight.

Danny smiled at her and said 'goodnight'.

Danny waited until he heard footsteps upstairs, then turned back to Mike and raised his glass. Mike did the same back to him. 'What are we drinking to?' he asked.

Danny thought about the question for a second

then answered 'To family'.

'Okay then' Mike said, 'To family' He reached his glass across and clanked it against Danny's. Both men took the glass down in one gulp. Mike reached for the bottle and pulled the top off and poured the same again for each glass. When he finished pouring, he replaced the cap and put his large hands back around the glass. He looked up at Danny and said, 'I know why you're here Danny.'

Danny stared back at him for a moment, then answered. 'I'm here to say hello to you and your family.'

'Not here at my house' Mike said 'Here, as in back in Boston.'

Danny tapped the top of his glass with his index finger for a few seconds before answering. 'I'm not going to bullshit you Mike. Of all people, I won't bullshit you.'

'I know you won't Danny. So what's your plan?'

'I guess I don't have much of plan really. I just can't fucking walk around anymore like everything's cool. Jim's fucking killer is walking around free like shit never happened.'

'I didn't realize you were walking around playing things cool. Seems to me you've be hotter than Mel fucking Gibson since it happened. Michelle still calls Elaine every so often. She doesn't paint a good picture of you Danny.'

'Yeah well, she'd fucking know I guess Mike. Things just got out of hand I guess, I don't know.' Danny paused and took a gulp from his glass. He looked back up at Mike. 'I ain't asking you to help or anything man. I know you got bigger things to worry about.'

'Don't you Danny?' Mike answered 'What's going after McBride gonna solve? It sure as shit ain't bringing Jim back.'

Danny felt hopeless. He knew Mike was right, but he refused to accept it. He leaned his face against his folded hands on the table and bit down on his thumb. After a second, he popped his head back up and said. 'I have to fucking do something man. He was my brother. I owe it to him to do something.'

Mike didn't answer with words. He finished his drink and poured another into his own glass and topped off Danny's. Once it was poured, he put the bottle down again, picked up his glass and took it down in one gulp. He got up from his chair and started towards the hall door. He turned back towards Danny before leaving. 'The central heating upstairs is very loud, especially when the doors are shut Danny. It'd be a shame if someone was to ever bust through the back door and rob me.' He nodded again at Danny 'Goodnight brother.' He said, then turned and walked through the hallway.

Danny heard his footsteps as Mike climbed the stairs, then he heard the bedroom door shut. He knew Mike didn't want any part of what he planned to do, but at the same time, he knew Mike couldn't let him go empty handed either.

Danny finished his drink and washed out the glass in the kitchen sink. He tip-toed back through the house and grabbed his coat, hat and gloves then went back to the kitchen. He turned the lights off in the kitchen and turned off the back porch light. He then put his coat and gloves back on, and pulled the tight winter hat back over his head.

He walked out the backdoor and pulled the door shut. He checked that it was locked. He walked down the steps and looked into the bed of Mike's pickup truck. Inside he saw a black iron flat bar left loose next to a pile of empty cans. Making sure his gloves were pulled on tight, he reached over and grabbed the tool quickly. He walked right back up the steps to the back door. As quietly as possible he jammed the flat bar into the door jam and with one quick pop of the lock, the back door broke open. Once inside the kitchen, he opened a number of draws and cabinets to make it look like someone searching for cash. In a cabinet above the refrigerator he found a coffee can full of money, mainly rolled up twenty dollar bills and emptied out the contents. He stuffed the cash into his pocket and rolled the can onto the floor. Next he headed directly to the liquor cabinet. There was a dummy block of wood that served as a trapdoor to a secret compartment. He looked inside and there it was, same as always, Mike's 9mm pistol, which he often brought over to the Braintree gun club to fire off rounds to blow off steam. It wasn't loaded, but Danny reached up high over the top of the cabinet and found the stack of bullets. He popped the clip from the gun and loaded it with bullets as quickly as he could manage. He wasn't experienced with guns really, so he fumbled one or two shells and had to go onto his hands and knees to find them and pick them off the floor. Finally, he stuffed the gun into his deep coat pocket, then walked quickly out of the house through the back door and down towards the main street.

He moved as fast as possible without bringing

obvious suspicion. If anyone saw him, he wanted to appear to be walking briskly to shrug off the cold. He was sweating pretty heavily with fear and with the increased body heat from his walk by the time he got back to the train station.

The train thankfully came within minutes and he walked onto the car and took a seat by himself, trying his best to look nonchalant. While sitting, he could feel the weight of the gun in his pocket sitting on his thigh. He prayed silently that the thing wouldn't go off by mistake and blow his dick off.

Wollaston T station was only 3 stops away, but the trip felt longer than his flight home to Boston. He stood just before the train stopped and walked onto the platform at Wollaston. The bright lights blinded him when he stepped off the train and he squinted until his eyes adjusted, moving slowly and trying to avoid bumping into anyone. He was filled with fear that if someone bumped into him, they'd feel the gun in his coat and he'd be forced to run, undoubtedly drawing attention to himself. He walked down the steps from the platform and through the exit barriers. He took a right at the bottom and headed up the steps towards Newport Ave, then stopped at the cross walk and waited for the lights to change to red.

He knew where McBride was staying. It was the same place many Quincy ex-cons stayed when they were paroled. It happened to be a block away from the house Danny grew up in on Farrington Street. He'd visited his father there on a few occasions, so he knew the layout and how it operated.

When the light turned red, he crossed Newport Ave and continued onto Brook Street past the old DeeDee's lounge and a Carpet Warehouse. He took the second right and turned down Farrington Street. The darkness of this street used to haunt him on walks home as a young teenager. For some reason the street lights in that part of Quincy were spaced too far apart. Many nights, he actually jogged home down this street because it gave him the creeps so badly. This night however, he needed the darkness, it covered his intentions from any neighbor up later than usual that happened to glance out the window and check for snow falling. He still felt the fear however. His heart was filled with fear . . . and with doubt. Mike's words had meant something to him of course. 'Why shouldn't they?' he thought. 'He's right. Jim's not coming back no matter what happens to McBride.' But he made his decision and it was final, regardless of the consequences. Flynn McBride was going to die.

Either he was going or Danny felt like he'd be the one to go. 'What difference does it make to anyone now?' he thought. 'They're all gone. I'm alone and that's not ever changing. Who would give a fuck if I'm gone?'

He bit his lip to chew back a sob. He felt tears well up in his eyes. They weren't for him however, they were for what should have been. They were for his younger brother, who didn't deserve what happened to him. They were also for those people he hurt from that point onwards. He thought just for a second that it'd best to just turn back, but as he considered it, he saw the halfway house only yards away across the small street. The house was pitch dark as were all the other houses on the block. He jogged across the street through a dark area not captured by a street light and snuck between the house's fence and a series of bushes. He ducked down low behind the bushes and waited for a minute to listen for footsteps both inside the house and around the perimeter. He edged his way closer to the side entrance and ducked low against a couple of garbage bins. He paused again for a breath and to listen to his surroundings. All he could hear was his own heart pounding through his chest. He heard it and felt it going like a jackhammer.

He tried to get his breathing under control, in

through the nose, out through the mouth, to slow his heart rate down. It worked after a minute and he slowly reached his hand into his coat pocket and pulled out the pistol. He heard a sudden bang behind him and turned quickly throwing his back against the wall and ducking his head behind the garbage can. His heart leapt back into overdrive. He saw a scar riddled cat move sleekly away from the garbage. 'It was the cat that caused the bang' he realized. 'Maybe only I heard it'.

He waited another minute for any other noises, but there was nothing. He decided to make his move. Staying crouched down, he slithered over to the side entrance and tried the door knob. To his surprise, it opened easily. 'Someone must've forgotten to lock it' he thought.

As had been the case when he'd come to visit his father there as a child, he saw the chart on the wall that outlined the 'guest' names and room numbers. He saw McBride's name near the top of the list and found the room number attached to it. He heard slight murmuring from upstairs, but figured that was normal, 'someone watching TV' he guessed. He slowly ascended the stairs, trying to keep the noise from the creaking steps to a minimum. He made it all the way up and paused outside McBride's room. He leant his ear close to the door to listen. The murmuring was definitely coming from his room, but he felt like it wasn't the TV. He swore he heard voices. Then he heard a loud thump, like a fist hitting a person's cheekbone. He knew the sound well. Someone was definitely in there, but he'd come too far to back out now he decided.

Danny took one last long deep breath and counted to three. Then he jumped to his feet and booted the door in with a loud bang and stormed into the room with the pistol raised.

He'd entered the room so quickly that the door had banged off the wall and slammed shut again behind him. He didn't say anything at first . . . not freeze or gotcha or anything. He just stared at the man's face that calmly turned to him when he barged into the room. It was a face he'd known well and thought about often, more often than he'd ever wanted to. It was his father's face, the Ghost, in the flesh, alive and well and standing in front of him. Danny felt his legs weaken, but he didn't buckle. His outstretched arm however did buckle under the weight of the pistol and the gravity of his discovery. He slowly lowered the pistol to his side, but kept his finger close to the trigger. His eyes moved down from his Father's face to his hands which were covered in blood and wrapped in a chain. The chain, he realized, was also caked in serum. He noticed a broad shadow in the darkness that eclipsed the rest of the room and knew it could only be McNulty. Then he looked behind his father to see Flynn McBride, tied to a chair, covered in blood and God knows what else.

One look at his target was all it took. Right away, he knew McBride would never live to see the light of tomorrow's sun. He wasn't sure what else he felt, the scene he encountered was unexpected and it was too troubling to comprehend in that moment.

Finally, Danny spoke. 'What are you doing Dad?' he said with a voice that sounded much younger than his thirty-plus years.

Billy Carson responded simply, 'I'm saving my son.'

'What?' Danny responded confused. 'Jim's dead Dad, you're too late.'

Billy shook his head. 'I have two sons Danny. I am too late for Jim, but not for you.' He stared into Danny's eyes long enough to see Danny realize what he was saying. 'Go home Danny . . . it's over now.' Billy said softly but firmly, and then he turned his back on his son and waited.

Danny was overcome with feelings too raw to understand. He stood for what felt like eternity staring at his Father's back and beyond to the heap of bloody mess that sat before him. Finally, he felt the gun slip from his gloved hand and heard it thump against the hard floor. He slid his feet backwards towards the door and reached for the doorknob twisting it open behind him. He turned at last and stepped into the dim hallway and staggered down the stairs and out the side door from which he'd entered. Outside, the darkness engulfed him like a quilt as he made his way briskly into the night.

EPILOGUE

'Mommy' the little girl with the dark curls asked her mother, 'where do the bunkies live again?'

'They're not bunkies baby, they're my *bunici*. It's the Romanian word for grandparents. Alex explained to her daughter. 'They live in Romania, near Bucharest.'

'Buuukaaaressst' the little girl repeated. 'Is that in America?' she asked.

'No, it's not honey, it's a different country. They moved back to Romania years ago.'

'Oh' the little girl said, nodding as if it was all coming together for her. 'We need to take an aero plane to go there right?'

'Yes baby, we do.'

'We're on an aero plane now Mommy. Does that mean we are going to Buuukaaaressst?'

Alex laughed gently and rubbed her hand through her daughter's wild hair. 'No Theresa, not this time. This time we're going to Dublin. Remember I told you we're going to visit your Daddy's brother Danny.'

'Oh yeah, I remember now Mommy.' The girl said and hugged her doll close to her chest.

Alex smiled sadly. She knew the awkwardness Theresa felt whenever the subject of her Daddy came up. Alex had done what she could to try to explain to the girl who her Daddy was and why he wasn't around. There's only so much you can explain to a 4 year old, even one so seemingly intelligent as Theresa. Alex knew that this would only get more difficult when Theresa began going to real school and making friends, most of which would have two parents.

'Come on baby' she said 'I want you to lay close to me now and get some rest.' She opened up the blanket and draped it over the child. 'We should sleep now and it will be morning when we land.'

'And we'll see Uncle Danny then.' The girl asked.

'Yes baby, that's right. We'll see Danny then.'

ABOUT THE AUTHOR

Paul Garvey was born in Boston. He moved to
Ireland in 2006 and currently lives in the Dublin area
with his wife and daughter. *Tomorrow's Sun* is his first
novel.

18205021R00139

Made in the USA
Charleston, SC
22 March 2013